See the way this shit goes
It's not as easy as it seems
But all you see is fancy cars, cribs and that green
And what blinded you were the haters called your
team
The bitches you would die for
And for them you would do anything
They backstabbed you and the killing part of all
You thought they were down
Yeah they was your downfall
But once you start learning you will see there is no
trust
Fuck a friend- fuck a nigga- Fuck a We-Theres no us
Loyalty is a bitch and it's hard to come by
Karma is a hoe and it will catch you by surprise
When you think you are good that's when shit gets real
The moment you get comfortable is when they plot to
steal
You don't even know they envied you the whole time
Sat right under you learned your moves and then tried
to steal your shine
But you be blinded by the fact that you thought they
were true
I'm a real bitch is what they told you
But fake is what you going to learn and what they going
to prove
And in the end it's just you
You gotta do – what you gotta do
Shamara Jackson

1

Copyright Page

THANK YOU

This book is dedicated to the one person who went to sleep lots of nights cuddled on mommies lap as she wrote. The one person that inspires me to take on the world and allows me to see the innocent soft side of life through his eyes. My number one fan my son Justin 'J.D'

I want to thank my husband Greg who always told me stop talking and start doing. Those words got this book done.

My mommy! My number one lady. You may not believe it but you give me energy and life. You always have the best advice and talks for me. You always shoot straight from the soul with the softest delivery. Often times it's not what you say but how you say it and mommy knows best! MUAH

To my sister De-De the ultimate hustler. My heart and soul. Your next up baby. I can't wait... It seems like our next chapter may be another journey together. You know I'm always ecstatic to have my life coach by my side.

Janell my 1st child, my baby sister & my 1st life lesson. It's ALL BECAUSE OF YOU. Remember that. You grew me up big time. Nobody knows or will ever understand our bond. That makes me smile. You are a great asset to this universe. I'm crying writing your part.

Iyisha my little big sister. You make it all seem so easy. I've always admired you. I'm very proud of you and you know why.

Sherida B. You did what I asked several people to do and that was read my product and be honest. You're the only one that came thru and I thank you!! Luv u

Sheila there was never any doubt about having your beautiful face grace this cover. I was your headache for 3 years and you never complained. I thank you for so much! Make sure yall go get #booked

4 years ago when everyone heard I was writing a book the outpour of support was amazing. Several times I gave up. I was tired of wasting money and just felt downright depressed. But due to having friends and family who don't let you forget your talents you're able to flourish. Y'all know who you are and what you mean to me. Sometimes we don't realize just how much support we have and love we receive from those that wish the best for us.

My best friends keep me going. Tera Talena Ticha & Madison. (In No Particular Order) My life without you guys? I don't want to imagine.

To the top we go!!! To the fans now and those to come, thanks for the support and all the love. May the universe be with you!!

FunnyMan
My Big Brother
We Miss You So Much
1/9/80-8/25/09
Continue to rest in peace

TEAM

CONCRETE

BY TOMISHA GREEN

PROLOGUE

Macy's department store loss prevention officers were spread out in the men's department watching their unknown perp. She piled Ralph Lauren Polo pieces onto the counter and had no idea that the local Macy's stores were onto her con. She had been to the State Street location on three different occasions, but she'd also been to three other Macy's stores in the Chicago area.

"Will that be all?" Meredith asked her. She was a trained fraud specialist for the store and posed as a sales associate to catch the thief at the register.

"Yes for today. I come here all of the time and I'm so glad that you've gotten new pieces in. My husband will love all of this."

"All of this is right," Meredith replied and started to ring her up. "This sure is a lot of Polo."

"Yes he loves it. He plays golf in it." The woman said and smiled. She planned to buy all of the men's clothing and then sell it on the street at a reduced price.

Meredith looked at the total of the pieces and smiled at her customer. "Will this be all? Right now you're at $875.29 with tax"

"Yes that'll be all," she said and pulled her prepaid debit card from her wallet. She swiped it into the panel available for customers to use, but the screen showed the word ERROR.

"Let me get your card," Meredith said. "My machine has been acting up all day," she said lying. She smiled because she knew that loss prevention had took over the register from their office and was in control of it. She swiped the card into her terminal and then asked the guest if she was using debit or credit.

"Credit will be fine."
The register processed the transaction and the purchase was approved.

"See what you've done Meredith. My husband is going to kill me."

"Oh really," Meredith said and looked at the receipt to compare the last four digits of the credit card on it to the last four digits on the card. They didn't match and Meredith knew that they had her. "I think your husband is going to be very mad at you. That's if you have one."

"What! That was rude. Just bag my things honey so that I can get out of here."

Meredith watched as her loss prevention associates grabbed the customer's arm before she said

"No, you're about to be bagged for fraud honey."

Violently the woman pulled away from the men and pushed one of them to the ground. She attempted to run, but another loss prevention officer tackled her and she slammed into a rack of neatly folded T-shirts. He pinned her down as another officer pressed his knee into her back.

"Get the fuck off me," she yelled and wiggled to get free.

Other customers looked horrified as the petite woman was pummeled by the officers. They watched her handcuffed and pulled to her feet, before dragging her across the men's department. The woman would not walk, forcing the officer's to be harsher than they anticipated.

"Ma'am please stand up and walk. We have you red-handed in this store, The Water Tower and Old Orchard stores using phony cards. The police have been notified, so just cooperate until they get here."

"Man ya'll don't have shit on me," she replied and stood up.

"We do and we know you're not the one making the cards," Meredith said as they walked onto the elevator headed to the security office. "We really need to know who made these cards you've been using."

"What?"

"You heard me ma'am. Who has been making these cards for you?"

"Let me just ask you this. If I tell you that can you let me go? I can't go to jail."

CHAPTER 1

Growing up Lynn went with everything her mother suggested and became a law abiding citizen. Mission completed up until she was kicked out of her old government job along with many other staff members. They had gotten the burnt end of the budget cuts and on that roller coaster of life she was at the bottom of the first drop. Within six months she had lost her boyfriend, home and sense of respect for the law. Taking a lower wage paying job was the only choice she had.

She parked her car in front of her sad apartment complex at 83rd and Grove Cottage. A bevy of young ladies played Double Dutch in a parking space and she prayed for them. *What would become of them in this hell hole*, she thought and frowned.

Lynn was a compassionate woman and determined to be an example for the youngins that grew up around her. Englewood was her home too and she often wondered what would become of her. She was 26-years-old and her future should be clearer, but it wasn't. "Not for much longer," she said as her sister hopped out of the car.

"What you say sis?"

"Oh nothing. I was talking out loud."

Most of what Lynn did was for her 16-year-old sister Janell. She inherited her sister when their mother was admitted to the crazy house for severe depression.

Janell was Lynn's heart and she planned to do everything to protect her and remain sane. She could not fall victim to the ghetto dynamics that had ruined their mother's life and had her locked away for five years now.

"Come here. Where are you going?" Lynn said to Janell as she walked away from the car.

"I am going over to Brittany's to hang out," she said and turned to walk away. She was a smart girl and earned great grades, but she had started to smell her arm pits or something because her attitude was becoming unbearable. She had even tried talking back, and Lynn had to lay hands on her. That happened once and Lynn assured her that she was going to act like a lady despite their surroundings.

Lynn walked up into her face and gave her a stern stare. "Listen here, you ask to go to Brittany's house. You're not grown to just come and go as you please. Do you hear me?" She had her hand on her hips, and did not stop looking her directly into her eyes.

"Yes, sis," she said and smiled. Her mini-me warmed her heart with her bright smile and big brown eyes. She knew what she was experiencing and wanted to rescue her from being a victim to their environment. The problem was she had already become a fighter.

Chicago had forced her to go from a sweet little girl to a fighting teenager.

Lynn was keenly aware of that and wanted to rescue her sister from being a victim of the windy Chicago streets. "I liked that apartment that we looked at and I hope that we get it."

"Me too," Lynn said and hugged her with all of her 200-pounds of thickness. If she was asked, she's too thick, but that was a lie. Lynn was perfect. "I am going to get us a three bedroom out of Englewood if it's the last thing that I do. I can't afford to lose you to the constant shootings here."

"I know, sis," she replied and she let her go. "I'm sorry about walking off. Can I go now? We're designing some T-shirts to increase the peace. I go to funerals all the time and I just gotta do something."

"That sounds much better.Bbe back in this house by eight and if you leave her to go anywhere you better text me."
"Yes," she said and walked away.

Lynn shut her car door and walked across the street to her apartment, which sat on the second floor of one of the buildings in the complex. She had just looked at another raggedy apartment in Englewood and could not take it anymore. She lived on the worse side of Chicago and was looking to move into a better part of the worse side. She laughed at the irony. The crime rate was amongst the highest in the country. She had no business living there, but after being canned by the government without warning it was the best that she could do. *Chaka Khan and Jennifer Hudson had roots here and if they made it, so the hell could I* she thought as her cell phone rang.

What the hell does this bitch want, she asked herself looking at the caller ID. She opened her apartment door, tossed her Old Navy handbag on the sofa and then answered the call.

"Nida, hey girl," Lynn said with the same excitement as a black bear growling at campers on his turf.

"Girl I just saw you ride pass me on Stony Island and 79th Street. What you doing over this side of town? You know it's crazy with the police looking for that boy that shot that lady last night." Nida was a messy woman that was in everything, but a coffin. She should be a hood news anchor because she always knew what's up in the town and it was the sort of subtle details that she asked Lynn about that kept her up-to-the-minute.

Lynn hesitated and thought about what lie she would tell. The last person that she needed in her business was Nida. After careful thought she realized there was no need to lie about why she was over on Stony Island. "I was looking at an apartment girl. You know how it goes, moving from one hood to another."

"Oh, really. Well bitch, today may be your lucky day. I may have the ultimate hook-up," she said and popped what Lynn assumed was gum.

14

Why is this bitch popping gum in my ear? She was not enthusiastic about Nida mentioning a hook-up. But she asked anyway. "What's that?" and then turned on the TV.

"Girl my uncle has the Section 8 hook up for $1500. He can get you a three bedroom voucher and you pay half now and the rest when you get your voucher in a week."

Lynn could definitely use a Section 8 voucher. She had gotten her tax return, and $750 would be perfect. *Shit, I could move out of Englewood if she came through with a voucher.* Lynn told her "I'm down," she said quickly without any further thoughts. She grabbed her keys and dangled them so that Nida heard them. "In fact I am headed over to you now."

"Okay do that. Come to my crib," she said and then gave Lynn the address.

Lynn sent a text to Janell and told her to meet her at the BP gas station on the corner of their block to make a quick run. She was old enough to stay home alone for the half hour that she planned to be gone but with the way dead bodies piled up in Englewood she would not chance it.

* * *

Lynn sped to Nida's house and didn't care if she got a speeding ticket along the way. She could not miss that blessing and wasn't worried about any troubles with the law. She planned to deal with that when the time came. At that moment she had a responsibility to properly raise Janell. Lynn plotted to give her little sister all of the things that she didn't have growing up.

Once they arrived at Nida's house Lynn had Janell stay in the car. She jogged up to Nida's door it swung open, and she entered the apartment. Lynn immediately noticed new furniture and a lot of shopping bags scattered about the living room. She wanted to ask her about what was in them but decided against it. Nida loved to gloat and as down as Lynn was she may have kicked her ass for making her feel less than a person. Lynn was jealous at the moment but she could not let Nida get a hint of that. She was actually shocked that she had shared the Section 8 lick with her because she was often very selfish.

"How you been Lynn?" Nida asked and had a seat on a leather sofa. The smell of it was fresh.

"I'm great. Just trying to make a better life for my sister. You know me. That's all this shit's about." Lynn had a seat and was being sincere with Nida. She subliminally let her know why she was willing to commit a crime. Lynn needed Nida but she was certainly a boss. Some people that didn't earn the title boss and it seems as if everyone was called that and Lynn hated it. The terms boss and hustler were used to loosely for her. Lynn was always in charge and took care of business though. She knew how to placate people and let them think what she wanted them to as long as she gained what she wanted.

"Okay I hear that. Well as you can see I am doing well for myself," Nida said and waved at all of the bags lining the wall. "I just shop all day," she said laughing.

I don't give a damn, bitch, Lynn thought and dug into her purse for the money. "Well, let me get out of your hair and let you get to shopping." She handed over the money and then asked, "So I should have the voucher in about a week and I can go looking for a place now right?"

"Yup," Nida said and counted the money. "We're all good. I will text you as soon as the voucher comes in."

"Cool," Lynn said and stood to leave. "I'll be waiting on you to come through Nida" she said as she opened the door. She wanted to make it clear that she looked forward to the move.

"Girl I got you. It's as good as gold. When I did it the girl had it ready in three days. Go ahead and find you a fancy place because this is in the bag."

Lynn was excited to learn that this had already worked for someone else. She said, "I know your mom was glad that you moved out." I laughed and hugged her.

"Fuck you," she replied and then gave me the middle finger.

"I'll talk to you later then hun," I told her and left her house happy for the moment.

*   *   *

17

After dropping the money off to Nida, Lynn immediately began looking for a three bedroom home in Chatham. Chatham was one of the 77 areas on the South Side of the City of Chicago, Illinois.

Its residents were overwhelmingly middle and upper income African American and it was home to former Senator Roland Burris. It was a much better area than Englewood and closer to Lynn's receptionist job.

Six hours and five apartment visits later, Lynn finally found one that was right up her alley. She had lied and told the realtor that her voucher was in the mail and she could go ahead and schedule for an inspection in a week. The woman looked skeptical but Lynn couldn't lose the chance to rent the place.
"I don't think that it works that way..." the woman began to say.

Lynn pulled money from her wallet and counted off money. "I tell you what ma'am. Let me give you $500 to hold off showing the place to anyone else. Just a little reassurance that I am confident that the voucher will be here within a week."

Lynn blinked her eyes and looked saddened. "Please," Lynn said and looked over to the car where Janell sat playing on her cell phone. "That's my little sister. Our mother is in jail and I just want to save her from the inner city violence and drama. She's a good girl and deserves the best. Just please help me. One week."

The woman tossed her clipboard into her briefcase, and said, "I can do that."
Lynn smiled.
"One week."
"Thank you."

CHAPTER 2

Over the next few days Lynn patiently waited for the voucher, but the loud neighbors had reminded her that she had to get out of there. It was 7 in the morning and while she was getting ready for work the noise was a pain in the ass.

"Janell you ready." Lynn yelled towards her sister's room. She had been taking her to school so that she only had to take public transportation one way.

"I been ready," Janell said and walked out of her room. She wore jeans a button-up and a cute cardigan. Headed for the door she said, "I need some money today if you have it sis."

"What for?" Lynn asked walking out the apartment door. She locked it and waited for a response.
"I want to pay a fee to try out for cheerleading."

"Oh okay that's cool babes.You'll look real cute in the cheerleader uniform too."

"Yup I can't wait. I'm going to kill it," she replied smiling knowingly and hopped in the car. One thing I love about her is her self esteem.

Lynn headed down the Stony Island and after a few blocks passed by the Jackson Park Hospital and Medical Center.

"Is that boy Jason still in the hospital?" Lynn asked passing 75th Street.

"Yes, it's so sad. So many of the guys that I know have been shot or killed. We gotta get out of Chicago. One day I am going to get rich and get us out of here."

"That's what I want to hear. Just stay..." Lynn was startled by a man that darted out in traffic. She swerved the car around him and slammed her hand on the horn. She rolled her window down, and yelled out, "You stupid bitch." She was pissed to no end as she made a slight right onto Cornell Avenue.

"As I was saying before that asshole almost had me in jail for killing him, just stay focused and we're going to get out of here. I promise you that."
"Yes I am. You don't have to worry about that. What's up with the place we're moving to in Chatham?"
"I am going to call Nida today and ask."

For the rest of the ride Lynn drove along Lake Michigan, and imagined how her life would be if only she had access to more money. Her motive was to care for herself, but she envisioned the things she'd do for her family if she had it. Something had to give for her. The Section 8 voucher was a start and it was up to her to make more happen.

The 17 minute drive from their home to Pershing Road and Martin Luther King Drive was an eye opening one. Both ladies had time to reflect on what the future had in store. Lynn pulled over and told Janell to have a great day at Phillips Academy High

School. They were a few blocks from the school because she didn't want to drop her sister off on school property as if she was some little girl.

"Here's the money for the team," Lynn said and smiled. "And what are you going to wear to this prom girl?"

"I will go and look for a dress one more time. I still have time to get one made too and I am not on the team yet."

"Oh, but you will be. All the pretty girls make the team." Both sisters laughed and they parted ways.

Lynn continued on to work and called her cousin Reggae. She was a true fashionista and needed a fashion consulting business. Everyone ran to her for advice on what to wear and how to wear it. It was a natural gift.

On the fourth ring, Reggae answered. "Bitch, what the hell you want at this time of morning. You know I was up half the night."

"It's an emergency," Lynn said and laughed. They were close cousins and helped each other as often as they could.
"What is it and you better not be playing? You know I need my beauty sleep."

Many people regarded Reggae as bourgeois. People that really knew her would swear that she was

simply confident in a city that didn't encourage young
ladies to have grand self-esteem.

"We have to get Janell ready for her prom.
She's clueless."

"We," Reggae said and laughed. "You're her
sister slash mother," she said and laughed. "You take
care of that."

"You know what..."

"You know I got you." She was cracking up with
laughter. "She gotta be the baddest chick there so I am
all for helping." Reggae stayed checking out the
Internet and magazines. She knew all of the hottest
and latest trends.

"Thanks so much. With all this trying to move
and shit my mind is just not into that. I can't worry
about her well-being and no damn prom."

"Sure you can," Reggae replied and stopped
laughing. "Parents do it all of the time."

"News flash, I am not a parent. I am too young
for this. But I am doing it."

"Yes, you are and don't worry. It's going to all work
out. You're a good person. People like you always
have great luck."

"I hope so. And I hope I get that damn
voucher today. I am tired of that damn apartment."

"It's gone come. You at work, yet?"

"Yup I just pulled into the parking lot. Let me hit you back later."

CHAPTER 3

"Thank you for calling Matsuda Construction," Lynn said in the telephone at her job. She didn't like being a receptionist much but it took care of her. She directed the caller to the sales department and went back to sorting the mail.

She looked at her nails and thought, *damn I need a manicure.* She worked hard but trying to maintain her life and take care of her sister was taking a toll on her. She had to do what she had to do at that time and wished that going back to college was an option.

Normally her cell phone was turned off because the last thing that she needed was to be sidetracked by social media or text messages from one of her best friends. The phone had lit up and she looked at the text message.

Janell: Lynn you have to come get me.
Lynn looked at the screen and the first thing that she thought was that her sister was in danger. She would be in jail if someone bothered her sister.
Lynn: What's up??
Janell: Getting suspended for arguing with a teacher. She brought up that Mom was in jail and I went off. I should have beat her ass
Lynn: I am on my way.

Lynn tossed the phone into her bag, powered down her computer and then walked to her manager's office. She knocked on the door lightly and was qued to enter.

"I am sorry to bother you," she said and then added

"I have an emergency and have to leave. My sister needs me at school."

"What's the problem? Who will answer the phones?"Asked Sue. She was a quiet Japanese-American that ran a tight ship.

"Well, I'd rather not say what has happened at school until I find out."

"I'm sorry; if it's not an emergency then you can't go. We need the phones answered and your other duties. No one here can do them."

"I know, but my sister needs me and I am not sure if it's an emergency. Can I just go check it out and come back?"

"Lynn I cannot do that. If you leave to check it out then I'm afraid you don't have to come back. In fact you can't."

Lynn stood there for a second frozen in time. Did this little bitch just fire me, Lynn thought. They never wanted any black people working here any damn way. I don't need this racist bullshit.

"Okay, fine. I won't be back. My family is important to me, just like your family means the most to you. I can't just leave her there. People are being

26

killed here every damn day, so it's always an emergency. I can't believe you're firing me."

"We have a business to run here, and need someone that doesn't have home problems here." Was her only reply without even looking up.

"You're an asshole," Lynn said and walked out of the office. She had a more important matter to deal with and she'd find another job someway.

CHAPTER 4

Courtney Edwards walked out of the blue-line train at the Monroe Street Station. She walked passed a few stores as she crossed State Street headed to the United States Probation Office. Since her arrest at Macy's she hadn't been anywhere near State Street. There she was walking into the probation office for the Northern District of Illinois. She passed through security and frowned as she walked around to suite 1500. Ex-cons and other people on pre-trial probation sat around the lobby area waiting to be harassed by their probation officer.

She approached the bullet proof glass and told the reception clerk that she was there to see Judith Kennard. After a half-hour wait Judith came out and gestured for Courtney to join her. She took her into a little room with a metal detector and checked her again as if the security at the building's entrance wasn't effective.

"So how are you?" Judith asked, and smiled. She was a cheerful, jovial woman that loved her job.

"I am not too good. I really can't believe that I have gotten myself into this," Courtney replied as they walked by Judith's office. "Where are we going?"

"To an interview room. There's two Secret Service agents here to interview you."
No they're here to get me to rat Courtney thought and frowned. What the hell have I gotten

into?

CHAPTER 5

Lynn and Janell walked out of the school and Lynn was pissed, but kept her cool. She tried her best to have patience with her sister who had a violent streak that she knew all about. They talked about the incident at school and then Lynn confessed that she was fired. They went into the house laughing.

"You're kicked outta school and I have no job. We're the best," Lynn said and both ladies cracked up with laughter. The absurdity was funny, but it was no laughing matter.

"I know right," Janell replied and turned on the TV.

"Let me call Nida, so I can see what's up with us getting the hell out of here." Lynn walked to her bedroom and threw herself onto it.

She called Nida and didn't get an answer. Sitting her phone on the bed Lynn shimmied out of her blouse, pumps and dress pants. It had been a while since she was home that time of day on a weekday. She slipped on some jeans that hugged her hips and a cute T-shirt that read: Sittin Pretty. She picked up her phone and tried Nida again.

*   *   *

Lynn had called Nida several times and she did not answer. *This hoe is ignoring me* Lynn thought. *What the fuck was up? I need to calm down, but I am going to keep dialing her number until she answers.* What pissed Lynn off more was that Nida hadn't answered her phone calls or text since the day she dropped off the money for the voucher. Lynn just wanted to shoot the breeze with her, but that never happened. Lynn didn't want to think the worse, but she was out $750 and being ignored.

Calm down, Lynn.

Think girl.

Think.

After a few moments to clear her head Lynn decided to call Nida's mother's house. She knew she had moved out but perhaps her mom could help her. Nida sometimes acted like a big ass kid, although she was twenty-seven with three college degrees. You'd assume that she knew how to return a phone call. Good or bad news. She acted like a kid and talked too much which was why Lynn had never got close to her. She was a great associate though.

Ms. Hernandez, Nida's mother was the sweetest woman. She and Nida barely got along and Lynn didn't know why. Lynn wondered why she hadn't thought of calling her earlier.

"Hey baby, how you been?" Ms. Hernandez spoke in her broken English. Nida was born in Chicago but her parents were from Mexico.

"Hey, Mamacita. How have you been?" Lynn asked genuinely.

"Other than bills, baby I been fine."

31

"Ha I can attest to that. Ma, is Nida around?"

"No baby. I haven't seen her since this morning. She went to go see her uncle John up at Brogan High School. He's the basketball coach over there."

She had unknowingly gave Lynn her brother's information. Enough to locate her $750 anyway.

"Okay Mama H, I'll try her cell. Thanks so much mami." Lynn said and happily hung up. She then immediately searched Google for the number to the school. She dialed the number once it came up, and was greeted by the voicemail of John Hernandez. She left a message as if she were a concerned parent and hung up.

*　　*　　*

Within an hour, John had returned Lynn's phone call. She calmly explained who she was and her dilemma. He chuckled and told her to meet him at the school in an hour to chat. When she arrived John met her in the parking lot of the school. He explained to her that Nida gave him the money, but the girl at the office had become afraid to pass along the fraudulent voucher.

"She heard a rumor that someone was being investigated for passing the phony vouchers and is now afraid to do it," he said and bounced a basketball on the ground.

"Okay so let me get my $750." she said, and crossed her arms over her chest. She didn't want to hear anything else. *Just give me my money before I have my people up here to pop your top*, she thought.

"Baby girl, you can either take your money back or I can keep the $750 and tell you how to turn it into $7500," he said and raised an eyebrow.

Lynn was always up for making extra money, but the problem was he had already failed to deliver on the promise of one lick already. She leaned her head to the side and squinted her eyes before she said,

"Let's hear it?"

He put his arm around her and said "Lets walk and talk so I can put you down."

Over twenty minutes he told her about a game that would sky rocket her life to another planet. It could also crash her back to Earth several times over, too. How she'd come out was the question Lynn struggled with most. She thought for a moment and after careful thought she left without her $750.

Lynn drove home in deep thought. John had given her more than an earful and it was some serious business to make money. She had never heard of anybody doing that kind of thing, so she knew it had to be kept under wraps. *I could not work alone though,* she thought. She thought long and hard about who she could trust to help her pull the job off. She hit the people closest to her. And those who deserved to eat. She called them and told them to meet her at her house in an hour.

33

CHAPTER 6

John walked out of the William J. Bogan Computer Technical High School and strolled along 79th Street. He was headed to meet one of his best workers and was excited. He saw her car parked in the Walgreens parking lot across the street from the school at 79th and Pulaski Road. She sat on the hood of the car like a fox. John thought that she was perfect and if he wasn't married he'd make a move on her.

When he reached her he held out his arms and gave her a friendly hug and grinned. He said "I see you're back for more quicker this time."

"Yes I need to save up some more cash. I need like $20,000 to get out of the Chi. I want to head to the west coast," she replied and passed him an envelope. "That's $3,000 for 100 cards. I need that many because I plan to sell them and get me some runners."

"Finally, "he said and put the envelope into his back pocket. "I told you a long time ago to get you some workers."

"Well, now I am ready. I am on a mission," she said and smiled. Courtney knew that the feds sat in the BP gas station parking lot across the street from them and listened to their conversation with the wire that had fitted her with.

"Yeah I see. I have a new recruit too. She may have a few work of her friends working with her. I gave

34

her a good deal since she came in with the workers. I am going to give you 125 cards for this money because I fuck with you like that," he said. *I also want to fuck you so maybe this gift will get me closer to that prize,* he thought.

She walked around to her car door and said "Thanks," while smirking.

*   *   *

Secret Service Agents Jennifer Dixon and Gloria Jackson were in the BP gas station parking lot at the corner of 79th Street and Pulaski Road. They had a great view of the conversation between John and Persia.

Agent Jackson was a woman of Indian and French decent and her long luxurious hair exuded her heritage. She was 35 and a lifelong member of the force. What was perfect about her was that she looked much younger and often was able to blend with college crowds to get information on counterfeiting and other theft related crimes. She had a cell phone camera pointed at her two subjects and snapped many photos of them. John's arrival, the hug and the money exchange was all snapped.

Agent Dixon had her cell phone camera recording the incident at the same time. She was a plus-sized White woman that had a great sense of humor. This was her second case that she had employed a confidential informant. She took her wins

35

anyway that she got them but was aware that the time would come when she wouldn't get any insider help.

"A gym teacher stealing and selling credit card numbers to duplicate. That'll be the ABC channel 7 headlines when they break this story," Agent Dixon said and smiled. "As soon as he passes her back the stuff we're getting a tap on his phone and the gym office phone."

"Maybe," Agent Jackson said and put her phone away. "The coach phone may be off limits if other people use it. We can't infringe on their liberties trying to catch our perp."

"What a shame because they may all be involved."

Pulling out of the parking space, Agent Jackson said,

"And we will get all of them."

CHAPTER 7

Orange painted walls were lined with funky pictures of Black musicians in Lynn's living room. They were one of the things that she had managed to get from her mother's home before she was arrested. She had a dark brown sectional and ottoman that sat on a cute rug, which gave her living room an autumn feel. Lynn liked the colors of the fall and that theme inspired her living room decor. Her friends had arrived and she was ready to chit chat with them about being on her team.

Lynn walked out of the kitchen with a glass of juice and sat on the arm of the sofa. She looked out of the window at Cottage Grove and hoped this new lick would finally get her off of it. She wasn't holding her breath because she had just been let down and wouldn't be fooled twice. She looked at her girls gossiping and unselfishly hoped that they all made it out of the hood. She took her keys and banged it on the glass and everyone looked at her.

"Who the fuck you thinking you are calling a meeting to order, bitch?"Reggae said and fell into laughter.

Everyone laughed and looked at Lynn like she was the head of a new organization being formed. She had invited Tru, Nikki and Reggae to join her. They sat stoically around the living room and waited for her to fully explain why she invited them there.

"Yes do tell since you had us all rush over here," Nikki said and gave Reggae a high five.

Lynn smiled because she knew that they were excited to finally get some real money in their pockets. They had their own things going on, but a bitch could always use extra free money.

"I'm going to get right to it and tell y'all that Nida didn't come through on the voucher."

"Oh so we going to beat that ass," Tru said, and then added, "You ain't even have to get all of us here. I could go and handle that for no money, if that's what you called a get money scheme in ya text to come here..."

The girls all nodded and expressed their points on Nida not giving Lynn the voucher.

"Well no I didn't get the money back, but I came up on a lick that we all can make money from. As much as I'd like to fight her it ain't even worth the trip to Cook County."

"Okay so what's happening?"Tru asked.

Lynn was being too mysterious for. Tru seemed to have a little attitude. She was as cool as they come but sometimes she just didn't not care about the average things normal people care about. She was down but just wanted to get to the bottom line. She was the dictionaries definition of 'I don't give a fuck'.

"I met up with her uncle who was supposed to pass off the voucher from his girl. He was going to give me my money back, but instead he made me an offer. I accepted."

"And that was?" That was Tru again.

"Dude gave me two Visa Gift cards with no name. They have the Visa logo so we can use them as credit cards anywhere that we want. He said just go to the mall or anywhere and use the cards to buy whatever I wanted. He told me to make sure that I triple my initial investment of $750, which I let him keep from the Section 8 situation."

"This sounds a little too good to be true Lynn, and scary," Nikki told her. Nikki's love for expensive clothes that fit her short bodacious frame had peeked her interest. She was a twenty-three year old fire-cracker and respected the game, but she didn't want to get into trouble.

"I know it does, but he did warn me that I had to worry about the info not matching up. Basically swipe the cards at places that allow customers to do it so the cashier doesn't see the card. From what he told me there is a machine that will allow you to add different credit card numbers onto another card via the magnetic strip.

The reason you have to be careful in the store is because the credit card number on the front of the card will be different from what actually prints out on the receipt."

"I get it. Whatever numbers you added to the strip is going to print out on the receipt. So if the cashier matches the last four on the card to the last four on the receipt, we have a big problem right?" Reggae asked.

Lynn clapped her hands and said "Bingo Hun. That's exactly how it goes. Even the expiration date is off so you have to be careful. I doubt if cashiers are hip to this because he said no one else is doing this kind of credit card shit yet.
He going to hit me with the machine and everything like the laptop and disks needed to hold the credit card info so all I gotta do is get new credit card numbers emailed and he can get his cash through a Western Union transfer. That way he and I never have to be seen together again. It's that simple and I really think this is it. We need this to happen. I say we because there is no way that I can come up without my girls."

Tru said, "Bitch, how can we make money shopping?" She was a smart mouthed 24-year-old that stood 5'5 with all hips and no stomach. Tru was skinny but not too skinny. And if Lynn ever needed shoe advice she was the girl to hit up; her shoe game was crazy.
Reggae was always quick on her feet and fast with her tongue.
"You can probably save some cash now on your shoes," she said to Tru and started laughing. They all started laughing too. They were loud.

"I don't get the joke," Nikki said looking puzzled. She had a frown, so Lynn guessed she didn't find it funny.

"OMG," said Tru, and then added, "You are so slow."

"I meant if we can shop with other peoples credit card info then instead of spending cash on all them damn shoes you can swipe away and save your money," Reggae explained to Nikki patiently.

"That actually goes for all of us." Lynn pointed out. "You can shop anywhere credit cards are accepted. So the more comfortable you feel then the more you can swipe."

"Yes Lord, shopping gives me life," Reggae said and smiled.

Tru didn't think it was funny. "I'm serious," she said.

"Look, credit is like cash. We can buy shit with the cards and keep our cash. There are tons of ways to get paid. For instance buy some iPods, computers, or TV's and sell them. Hell, take a bitch to the store. They can get what they want, and then give you cash after you take a little off. He gave me two so we all 'bout to shop off these and get a feel for what's what. I am not greedy.

We should be able to get some fresh clothes and make money to send him more money to do it

41

again. Since me and Reggae are the only ones with bank accounts and swiping experience we'll split up and hit different places. Tru you with me. Nikki you with Reggae. Let's hit Ford City Mall since its closest to us and Best Buy. Get some laptops and nice clothes," Lynn said.

"What about Viv and Renee? Why you didn't call them over?"Asked Tru. Viv was Lynn's cousin and Tru's sister.

"No bitch," Lynn said and balled up her face. "I am 26 and doing what I want. They are in high school and I am not messing up their futures with this. I do have a heart and some common sense. This is their last year and right now they're too young. Let them go to college and do better than us."

"Yes," Reggae said. "I agree. Let's pick them up something in the mall, but they will not be doing this." She raised her brow to be sure Tru got her point. She was pissed that Tru even suggested that.

"Let's split and meet back here in three hours. Be careful y'all and don't be greedy. Greed always gets people caught. Run if you have too." Lynn said jokingly. They all laughed and headed out of the house.

CHAPTER 8

Lynn pulled off and they made their way towards Cicero Avenue. She and Tru were jamming to DJ Pharris on Power 92.3. The sun shone brightly into the car and she couldn't see. She smiled and pulled down her visor.

"What are you smiling at?" Tru asked and turned down the radio.

"This sun was blinding me and I was laughing at the fact that I can't see my future after committing this crime."

Tru fell out in laughter.

"Bitch you better figure that shit out. Cause there is no room for doubt. You laid the plan out and I'm riding with you. I hope this shit really pop off so that we can get some money and get the fuck outta the hood."

Lynn pulled into a parking space at the mall nervous as hell. She had heard what Tru said and agreed, but had no idea what the hell was going to happen. Suppose she walked into a store and used the card and was arrested the very first time that she tried to use the phony card. So many would be disappointed and then what would she tell her sister. Who would take care of Janell at a time when she really needed a role model and someone to truly show her the way?

"Okay, here is the plan. In this plaza is Marshalls, and Old Navy. We can try it in these stores," Lynn said with optimism.

"Yes, and we can go to Chuck E Cheese's, too and buy gift cards. Hoes like to take their kids there for their birthday."

Lynn cracked up and got out of the car. "Girl, you are crazy."

*   *   *

Reggae walked around the Best Buy store with Nikki in tow. She wasn't nervous but the palms of her hands were sweaty. She needed the extra money and decided to purchase the merchandise for Lynn to resell before she got what she wanted for herself.

"So, what do you think we should get?" Nikki asked. "I know electronics, but I don't think we should buy a big ass TV because that'll take up a lot of car space."
"You're right," Reggae replied and then added, "Also someone may bust out my car windows while we are in the mall."

"Yes, we are going over to Ford City?"
"Of course, I want to hit Victoria Secrets and get me some jewels from Zale's."

"Yes," Nikki said and smiled. She looked around the large store and said, "You should get us laptops."

44

"No, we gotta get Lynn out the way."

"That's what I mean, Reggae. But we will pretend that they are for us so the sales clerk won't ask too many questions."

"Yes that makes sense. Let's do this so that we can hit Charlotte Russe."

After looking at the laptops, they approached a sales rep and asked for help.

"I can do that," the young sales rep said to them. He looked no older than twenty-one, and had a little peach fuzz growing on his chin. "Which ones were you looking at?"

"We wanted these Apple Mac Book Pro laptops right here."

He furrowed his brows and looked at them through squinted eyes.

"Two of these," he said and ran his hand across the laptop. "They are $1799 ma'am."

"We know," Nikki said. She seemed to be taking charge of the transaction.

"We're both headed to DePaul U in the fall and need them. Our parents loaded a gift card for us to get the best."

"Oh," he said and seemed relieved that they were not using a credit card.

"Let me head to the back and get them for you."

The sales rep disappeared to fetch the laptops.

"You think this it to high of a purchase," Nikki asked. She seemed concerned.

"No," Reggae said and curled her lips. "You really already sold it to him. You see it looked like he had an ah-ha moment when you mentioned gift cards. It's like he expected us to be using a stolen credit card or something."

"Right, here he comes now let's get these laptops and get the hell out of here."

CHAPTER 9

When Lynn arrived home, her car was filled with bags on top of bags. The number of bags made her scared to bring it all into her apartment. She didn't want her nosey neighbors all in her business nor did she want to be the victim of a robbery. She had already planned to say that her tax money had finally arrived to account for her new spending habit. Lynn was elated that she could save her money and shop with the cards to get the things that she needed for her and Janell. She was out of work and the whole time that she shopped, she contemplated what she would do next.

A few minutes passed and Nikki and Reggae pulled up with so much merchandise in the car, Lynn couldn't tell who was driving. *Damn damn damn. Fuck Section 8,* Lynn thought. *If this keeps up, I will have enough cash to live in a better area without any assistance from the government.*

Once inside the crib they all looked at each other and started screaming.

"I guess we need to start calling your boss now, huh bitch," yelled Nikki. She was very serious.

"Oh, no. No. Don't start that boss shit." Lynn warned them feeling overwhelmed but happy that everyone was safe.

"Now let's see what we got. Empty those bags," Tru said happily.

After they looked through the bags and split some things up, they agreed to meet again early in the morning. An hour was spent just showing off their fresh clothes and new shoes. It seemed like the only store Tru made it to was the shoe stores. All of them were beat, because they hadn't shopped like that in a long time. After going thru all of the bags they had charged roughly $8000 between two cards that only cost them $750. The merchandise was clothes, shoes and household things. Everything that was in the mall that day they had bought. They were hooked from the jump and Lynn liked that. They expresses that everything was smooth and seemed easy. Lynn told them to keep all their personal merchandise and give her the sell-ables.

* * * * *

Lynn sat on the sofa and stared out of her window at a group of hoodlums walking pass. She sent a positive message to the universe for the young black boys. She couldn't wait to get to an area that was quiet and serene. She closed her window blinds and decided to go take a much needed bath. Before setting her bed clothes out her phone rang and it was her brother Funnyman. He was calling collect from the county jail where he was fighting a murder case. Pressing Zero to accept the call the operator sang. He went right in.

"Man what the fuck you over there doing bitch?" He said laughing. His ass stayed calling us bitches. He knew we hated it coming from others but somehow he made it sound like it was our middle names.

"Fat ass. What's up? You outside?" I said back joking, wishing he really was outside.

"Man fuck you, call Pie!"

I knew it. His ass only wanted me to use my damn money to stalk his baby momma.

"Why the fuck don't I just put money on her phone since you always have me call her?' I asked.

"She not answering, the hoe mad like always." He said.

"Well she not going to answer for me either stupid!"

"See that's why Viv my favorite sister cause yo' ass hardheaded."

"You dumb fuck, Viv is your lil cousin. Just because you named her don't mean she your fuckin sister!" I replied back.

"She shoulda been my sister instead of yo slow ass. Look be up here tomorrow for court and text Pie for me. I gotta go back in for count. Yo stupid ass talked all my time up." He yelled.

"Aw you're so cute when you're mad. Aight Ill keep calling till she answers and see you tomorrow and good luck. Luv you!" I tried to squeeze all that in just before the fucking operator hung up.

49

In the morning she planned to let the ladies know that it was official and she wanted to work with them exclusively. The bath water ran into the tub and she thought about the different reasons why she chose the women that she did to work with her.

Reggae was her heart and Lynn couldn't imagine not eating with her. Tru was like her sister and she knew when it was all said and done she was going to ride with her until the end. That was how Tru got down; real thru and thru.

Nikki had been a part of their click since Tru drug her in one day trying to explain to her mom why they got kicked out of school. They argued and fought like crazy, but always had each other's back when it mattered. Nikki was family and she could be trusted without a doubt.

She planned on making a hair appointment for all the girls. Her friend Nyna owned a beauty shop called ENVY on Western. She had a beautiful set of twins named Mason & Messiah. She was a beast with hair, makeup and eyebrows. The girls deserved to look good and get pampered after today.

CHAPTER 10

It was no surprise that the ladies were on time to Lynn's house the next morning. She was getting dressed as they sat around talking and drinking mimosas. They were on the road to being classier than they already were, and their new lick was going to keep that image up. Everybody arrived looking brand new.

Lynn came into the living room and said

"Ladiesssss."

They all laughed at her chipper mood. She was wearing the new clothing that she had bought the day before. She was looking the part to go out and kill the stores again. Just looked like she farted out money.

"Okay, ladies I think we have something here. Last night I walked around my bags at least ten times before I hung that shit in my closet and took a bath. Ladies, I've always held a job but never have I been able to spoil myself like I did yesterday."

Tru said laughing, "And you finally look good."

They all screamed, "Yes," agreeing with Tru.

Lynn slapped hands with Tru, and then said

"So I have great news. I sold all of the stuff that y'all left yesterday." I went into my purse and pulled out a wad of cash. I fanned my face with the money.

"This is $2800 bitches. I had one of the dope boys come and buy all of the stuff. He said he knew some gay boys that always sold stuff and he plans to give it to them to get rid of it all."

They were all speechless.

Finally Nicki said, "This is so exciting. I can't believe that you've come up on this, Lynn."

"Me either," Lynn said and held her hand in the air. They all stacked their hands on hers like a sports team. "I know that y'all are all in. I know that we all plan to beat the pavement and we need a team name, so Team Concrete on three," she said and smiled. "One two three."

"Team Concrete."
They said it and all laughed and hugged. Team Concrete was born and they were ready to get that money.

"I have great news. I am getting the cards for $350.00 and not $750.00. So y'all go out and buy whatever y'all want but bring me back electronics and things to sell. We all have cards now also, so we do not need to split or personal stuff with our partners."

"That'll work," Reggae said.
Tru and Nicki agreed too.

Tru said, "I can't roll out with you today Lynn. I had an appointment set up before this happened.

"That's fine," Lynn said and then added, "If that's all, let's get this fucking money," Lynn said and walked her girls to the door and let them out. Tru looked relieved and left.

CHAPTER 11

After all of her friends left, Lynn sat on her sofa and stared out of the window into a dismal Chicago sky. It turned very dark outside suddenly and perhaps it was about to rain. She glanced at her purse that was open and saw the money in their and smiled. The money had brightened her day, and nothing outside of her family was going to ruin her spirit. That included the weather. Just as a few droplets of rain landed on her window, her cell phone rang.

"What's up boo?" She said into the phone. It was her close friend DeAnna from Texas.

Everyone called her Chill D because she owned a jewelry store. Well that and she was married to a cold-blooded killer so she had no worries. At 16 years old he served a seven year prison term for protecting his mom from an abusive boyfriend with a shot to his head.

"Hey cuz," she said and then added, "I wanted to know if you've gotten that voucher you were expecting. I don't like anyone taking advantage of you."

That's why she loved her, she was always calling to check on her.

She laughed. "No I didn't but you dont gotta go shoot anyone."

She chuckled and then said, "Well she didn't reply to me but her uncle did put me onto some scam that has gotten me a lot more money than that initial investment."

"Oh is that right? Tell me about that."

She hesitated. Could she talk over the phone?

"He taught me how to add stolen credit card numbers to gift cards."

"Wow Lynn. You're into that. I haven't heard about that one. You better be stacking your money, I know that."

"Yes of course. And I am getting me and Janell out of the damn ghetto. We have to get out of here."

"Okay I was just checking in on you. And be careful. They may not have alerted the stores there yet but I am sure the scammers are traveling."

There's an idea, Lynn thought. I could take this show on the road.

"Thanks, babe. I am going to be careful. I just have to get this money."

"And if you come across some jewelry..."

"Yeah. Yeah. I got you, but I am not trying to do too much. I like my freedom."

They both chuckled and hung up. DeAnna was definitely on the right path, by telling her to be careful. Chicago is known for everything and robbing you was one of em.

Lynn sat for a second and thought about the idea of traveling. What if they could do their dirt in smaller towns? It made sense to her because she had seen news broadcasts about robbery rings being caught on cameras. She didn't want her or the team to hit so many stores that they made the local news. People would definitely recognize them and call the police. If we flew to Miami and other fabulous cities and hit them, shipped the things home, and then flew back we would be good. What the hell am I thinking?

She thought and then chuckled. I need to get me a new job so that people don't begin to question me about my new found wealth. I do not want any trouble with the law, so I have to start being careful from the beginning of this. She placed a call to her close friend DeeA. She always had great advice and kept it real. She hated this lifestyle but as friends she has to accept it.

While calling DeeA,she grabbed her purse and then headed for the door. She planned to start buying decorations and things for her new home to come. Things were looking up and she was excited.

CHAPTER 12

FOUR MONTHS LATER

Everything was as Lynn had expected and some things were better. She had sent Janell on the perfect prom. Reggae had found her a nice high-end gown from one of the shops on the Magnificent Mile and Lynn rented a limo for her and her date.

Lynn was sitting on the patio at her new home in the serene Chatham area of Chicago. It was exciting and a new experience for her. The area was riddled with black folks like the south side, but these folks had a little sense. She had become a wiser criminal and ran her ring like a major corporation.

Lynn took masking her illegal gains seriously too. She didn't want to work for anyone, so she thought long and hard about what she could do for a small business. She thought of a party bus company, maybe an event planning business. Maybe some buildings to generate long term income. The ideas were endless. But right now it was stack time. And spend later!

Lynn sat in her small office area in her new home looking for shopping areas in the Milwaukee and St. Louis areas. All of the Chicago malls and the surrounding suburbs were her best friends. She and Janell used to wash clothes in the sink because they couldn't afford to go wash at the laundry mat. Now, they hadn't repeated the same clothes in weeks and

Janell and began to give them away to her friends at school. The best thing that Lynn had done was found a group of steady buyers that had milked her dry. She didn't have to sell to outsiders and that kept people out of her business. The buyers had long money and loved paying $500 for a $1000 TV. The money was piling up and none of her family and friends had any idea what she had been doing. She would occasionally buy them gifts and they liked that, but she did not want them in her business.

She and the ladies were focused on getting money and surprisingly they were not persuaded by the many men that tried to court them. They had bigger and better things on their minds and wanted to stack their money before they got into marriage and making babies. They were together so much that people may have assumed that they were seeing each other. Besides Chicago was a big city and its residents were not known for showing love to each other like Atlanta or New Orleans. The ladies feared that if they're scam got out they'd be a target for robbery or being turned in. Keeping the peace and being classy ladies was a top priority for Team Concrete.

There was a light knock on her front door and she saw Tru standing outside the screen door. She told her to come in and Tru did. She flopped on the sofa and tossed her purse to the side.

"Girl I am exhausted," Tru said and threw her arm over her face.

"What's going on boo?" Lynn asked and turned away from the computer.

"Well I haven't been up front with you cousin. I was almost arrested in the Prada store on Oak Street a few days ago. When the girl took my card to charge me she took it into the back room because they don't have registers on the floor. She came back out and told me that the four digits on the receipt and card didn't match."

"Well bitch you knew that. Like you knew better than going in any store that you can't monitor the transaction. You know better Tru."

"I know and I fucked up. That'll never happen again. The problem though is that the feds questioned me. I told them that I found the card and that I was sorry and they let me go. But I have to say that they had a folder and when they opened it, I saw a picture of the guy you've been getting the card numbers from."

"Get the fuck out of here," Lynn said and panicked a little.

"Yes, I don't know why. I think they were going to ask me if I knew him or some shit. But we have to be careful for now on. I know you're the leader in this and all, but I don't think that you need to be anywhere near him. And you need a new pre-paid phone to communicate with him."

"That's why I love you. I am definitely going to do that. I need to take care of getting that phone now.

Let's go to that Cricket store on Western Avenue now."

*   *   *

After they retrieved the phone Lynn mentally prepared herself to give John a call and let him know that she would be more cautious with her contact with him. She didn't know how he would take that but she was not trying to go to jail. It was now suspect that he kept trying to get her take over his business with the hacker. She always refused and now she was glad that she was not so greedy that she did that.

I don't know how much longer I am going to be doing this. She thought back to that scare she had in the Guess store downtown. The cashier still had the old imprinting machine and choose my card of all peoples to duplicate. After refusing and arguing back and forth she alerted the manager, who was more skilled and noticed the card wasn't right. I was immediately led to the back and police were called. Thankfully I had enough time to stuff everything in my pants so when I was searched they only found my id. The states attorney didn't want to pursue a case for a pair of jeans and two sweaters so they let me go.

CHAPTER 13

That evening Lynn sat in her bedroom on an iPad and looked at flights to different cities. She was interested in St. Louis and Milwaukee, but what she really wanted to do was go to Miami and Las Vegas. Sure she wanted to shop and make money, but she also wanted to have fun and enjoy the type of life that she was entitled to since she had the money to. Her plan was to book airfare and hotels for her and the girls and they would be out.

After looking at Expedia and Travelocity, Lynn found the perfect flights to Miami. She pulled out her laptop and opened her secured file that held all of her credit card numbers. She found an American Express number and paid for flights to Miami with and received her confirmation code without any problems. *Piece of cake*, she thought.

Next, she called her team and told them that she wanted them at her house the next morning by 6 a.m. They whined about the time, but when she told them what they were doing she had their attention. She warned them to bring only one carryon bag because she was taking her equipment and they would be working in Miami and shipping the things home. She got up because she wanted to see how her credit card making machine would fit into her bag. She had no intention of carrying it on the plane and through all of the TSA security. She needed it to go under the plan and she hoped that her bag was not randomly searched that way either. All she needed was to sneak away to a nice sunny place and bless it with her scam. Just as she wrapped the machine in bubble paper she heard the front door slam into the wall behind it.

"What the fuck?"

She said and raced down the stairs to the living room. She saw Janell looking wild and angry. Her hair was no longer neat and it was obvious that she had been in a fight.

"What in the hell were you fighting?" Lynn asked and followed her into the kitchen.

"I don't believe this shit."

"Lynn these bitches gone recognize now who the fuck I am. I aint no joke and I'mma stab one of these bitches."

"You ain't stabbing shit," Lynn said and locked the front door. She looked outside and saw about ten girls out there and two boys. "And you definitely ain't going back out there with all them, because you're going to have me get in that shit if they jump you. Now calm the fuck down."

Chapter 14

Not believing she was able to get up after last nights fiasco Lynn was relieved when all of Team Concrete pulled in front of gate A at the O'Hare Airport. They stepped out of the party bus, and Lynn

62

sent the driver on his way. They all had one bag and we're all dressed to impress. They stepped into the airport and Lynn approached the kiosk to print out their boarding passes. She entered the confirmation code that she had received from the airline the night before and it wasn't accepted. She was directed to head over to an agent to be assisted.

Lynn told the ladies that she had to see the agent to get their passes and asked them to wait where they were. They were fine with that because they had never flown on a plane and weren't excited about that. Lynn stood in the line, and then was called to the next agent.

"Hello, I was trying to print boarding passes for me and my family, but was asked to come over here."

"Sure, I can help with that," the agent said and then asked for Lynn's confirmation number. Lynn gave it to her and the woman tapped on her computer keys.

"Okay, ma'am do you have your ID?" She asked and then called over a supervisor.

"Yes maam right here, "Lynn said and passed her an Illinois driver's license.

"Thanks," the woman said and looked at it deeply.

"There seems to be a problem with the credit card used for this transaction. Do you have the card used for this reservation?"

Lynn immediately panicked. *Why would I be so stupid to use a stolen card to buy a ticket in my name? You're a dumb ass. Think. You better think fast or ya ass is going to jail,* Lynn thought. She said,

"My business partner who is not here, made our reservations. I don't have the card right now."

"Then I am sorry you won't be able to fly with this reservation," the supervisor said.

"O wow. Can I pay cash or use my card, which I do have?"

The two reps looked at each other, and then the supervisor replied, "Sure, that's not a problem."

"Okay," Lynn said and went into her large purse and pulled out a larger wad of cash. Thank the Lord, she thought. "What was the total again?" Lynn asked, and reminded herself that from that point on she'd only use cash for these kinds of transactions.

She paid the bill in cash and the agents handed her all of the boarding passes.
Lynn walked back over to her girls and handed them all their passes.

Reggae asked, "What happened over there that you had to cough up all that cash?"

"Yea two fucking thousand," Lynn groaned.She really wanted to cry. She pulled the girls in closer and whispered to them, "I used a credit card to make the reservation and it back fired. We cannot do that ever again. Always pay cash, y'all got that?"

They all agreed and started walking towards security.

"Now that's out the way, let's get to Miami bitches."
The ladies laughed and made their way to their gate to get out of the Windy City.

*   *   *

Just as the ladies walked off Secret Service Agents Jennifer Dixon and Gloria Jackson walked right up to the agent's that helped Lynn.

"Excuse me, I am next," another airline customer told the agents. "You have to wait your turn."

Agent Jackson flashed her badge, and then said, "Sorry, official busines, and we're next."
The man shook his head and then backed off.

"Hi," Agent Jackson said to the airline rep. "You just had a woman up here that brought several passes. Was there a problem?"

"It's funny you ask, ma'am, the rep said. "The credit card that she used came up as stolen. But because we can rarely see if the person actually made the transaction and then changed their minds we don't try to prosecute. She did pay cash for the flights."

"Well, we're investigating her and that crew for credit card fraud. Can we have all of their names? We will get warrants if necessary." Agent Dixon had a pleasant tone.

"Oh no problem, I kind of felt something was wrong. Then she had all of that cash. Seemed really fishy to me," the rep said and printed the boarding passes and handed them to Agent Dixon.

"Thanks, a bunch," Agent Dixon said and walked away. She stopped and then asked, "Who was the one that paid the cash?"

"Her first name was Lynn."

"Perfect," Agent Dixon said and then told her partner. "She paid so that's our leader."

"Without a doubt. We got them now."

"Sure do! let's go draw up warrants for the surveillance and Internet records to get the IP address that Ms. Lynn used to make the reservations."

CHAPTER 15

After being back from Miami a month later, things were starting to look even brighter for Team Concrete. Lynn couldn't be certain what the other girls were doing with their money, but she was stacking her money. She had started with $750 and about six months later, she had her home and was looking to settle on a four-bedroom unit for an investment. No one knew about it either. It was a surprise for the ladies and would serve as their headquarters. She had already dubbed it HQ and one of the units was set aside for preparing the cards, storing merchandise or just for the ladies to kick it.

Lynn was under the impression that the ladies would remain dedicated to the arrangement that they had. It was still as simple as them going out and buying whatever they wanted as long as they brought her back all of the hottest electronics. Although they couldn't complain, Lynn was starting to get a funny feeling from them. They had been to two trips over the last mont. Miami and Atlanta with Lynn paying for all airfare, rental cars, hotel rooms and dinner in cash. She wanted to be as accommodating to them as possible, but that was more for her well-being. She did not want the police knocking on a stolen hotel room door or accosting her the same way the airline agents did.

They were making enough cash to pay their bills and travel expenses in cash, and there was no need to risk their freedom. She had become so cautious that she had never met with her connect John in person. Besides he didn't want to hear about her extravagant shopping excursions, so they really had nothing in common but the money.

He simply told her, "Just run in the cash," and that was precisely what she had done. She was never big on fashion. Just nice cribs and cars. So far she has had a motorcycle, A Dodge Magnum & Now her Escalade. The rest of the crew seemed content with their fashion. She could only pray this wouldn't cause a rift between them. She always preached and acted like the mom, but you can only talk so much. What they did with their money was eventually up to them.

* * * * *

Lynn looked at the clock in her home and realized that it was 5 p.m. Although she hadn't had a 9-5 job in months that time meant something to her. She liked to head out to make her money at that time. The time worked perfect for her scheme. She would shop at stores and while chit chatting with stores clerks she would mention that she had just gotten off work and had been saving for whatever big ticket item that she was stealing. It worked perfect and over the months she had realized that the better the conversation with the store reps the easier it was to hand her over the goods.

She heard a car beep outside and her text notification on her cell phone went off at the same time. That was Nikki picking her up in one of the rentals that Lynn had out from Hertz rental car. She had set a business account with the rental company and all of her girls had vehicles.

Lynn text that she would be right out and grabbed her purse. She locked up her door and headed pout to meet her Mini-Me.

Nikki truly respected Lynn's hustle. She often spoke before she thought and she had a mean streak just in case anyone bothered her. Like Lynn, she had to raise her sisters while her mom ran the streets. It was times that she fought between her feelings of love for Lynn with her envious and jealous ones. She was a plus sized woman that dressed nicely with a cute face, but she was extremely self-conscious about her weight. She was a go getter that liked money and none of her personal problems had gotten in the way of that.

*   *   *

Nikki and Lynn were in the predominantly white working class neighborhood, Armour Square in Chicago. It was home to US Cellular Field, which hosted the beloved Chicago White Sox. The area also boasts Chicago's Chinatown, but that day it was Team Concrete's turf.

Lynn sat in the car and waited for Nikki to come out of Footlocker. She went in to get some Nike Foams for one of the dope boys that had made an order for them.

Nikki had the sales rep grab two pair of the sneakers and texted Lynn to let her know that she'd be right out. She paced around the store and her palms were sweaty which happened most times that she was about to commit a crime. She loved the money though, so she maintained her composure and made it happen.

"Ma'am, I am putting your shoes on the counter. They will take care of you up there," the sales rep that fetched the Foams told her.

"Oh, you're not ringing me up boo?" She asked with a flirtatious grin.

"No I can't," the young man replied. "I can put my number on the receipt for you though. I can't pull my phone out on the floor." He gave her a sly grin and a wink.

She laughed and said "We'll see," before walking to the counter.

"Are these your Foams ma'am?"A female sales rep asked. She was a Spanish older woman with some strong features. After scanning the items, she said "They're $250 each, so your total is $518 with tax."

"Okay," Nikki said and swiped her card into the credit card reader. She mentally crossed her fingers and hoped that the transaction approved.

It did.

The receipt shot out of the register and the sales rep grabbed it. She then asked Nikki to see the credit card and ID.

"I left my ID in the car but it's a prepaid card," Nikki said and flashed it.

"Oh, okay, I need to match the last four-digits of the card with the receipt."

Nikki panicked. She was stuck because she had never experienced that problem. Nikki handed the rep the card and prepared to tell her some lie about why the cards didn't match. She opened her purse to get her phone to text Lynn but was interrupted.

"These numbers don't match," the woman said and reached for her telephone.

"I have to call my manger about this."

"Um, don't worry about it ma'am. Just let me get my card back."

"I can't do that."

"What's the issue?"

"Just wait for my manager."

Nikki backed away from the counter and walked towards the door. When she got outside, she ran as fast as she could to the car. She swung the door open hopped in the car and yelled, "Drive Drive bitch hurry."

Lynn didn't know what happened, but she sped out of the parking space and out of the parking lot.
Nikki looked back and said, "Shit, the manager is outside. I think he's writing down the license plate number."

"G what happened?" Lynn asked speeding pass a few lights before hopping on the expressway at the 35th and Dan Ryan entrance. She looked over at Nikki whose big ass was trying to catch her breath.

"I think I hit them too much," Nikki managed to say through heavy breathing.
"She was like, stay here I'm calling the manager..." Nikki could not talk.

"Ugh, catch ya breath and tell me damn!" Lynn snapped. She was shiting bricks while Nikki attempted to catch her breath.

"My total was $500 Lynn and the shit went right through. The bitch didn't ask for ID until after the card had went through but I gave her the card after swiping it. She kept whispering to herself and then called the manager so I got out of there."

"You ran?"

"Yeah, I snatched the card and I jetted, G. Don't tell me that I should have stayed there and been calm mess either." Nikki was laughing as Lynn sped away from the crime scene.

"Bitch you're lucky this is a rental or they'd be at the door right now. It's all good. Shit happens." Lynn said but inside she was pissed. She knew that Footlocker was a done deal. She wouldn't be shocked if the store manager sent E-mails out to other stores.

"Shit we probably done with that store."
"That's cool. Its other shoe stores to buy Jordan's. But I also found these Foot Locker gift cards. They don't

have any Visa or MasterCard logo, but maybe we can use them."

Well at least she did that much, Lynn thought as a light bulb went off in her head. The Vanilla prepaid VISA cards were great, but she saw big things for the direct store cards.

"Let's get the rest of the stuff and get off these streets for today," Lynn said and then added "Let me warn everyone else to avoid that Foot Locker. Noll matter of fact avoid all of them. Those bitches probably alerted every store."

*   *   *

Two hours later, Nikki and Lynn were back at Lynn's home. Despite the Foot Locker scene Nikki was able to buy three lap tops with the touch screens. Lynn would sell those for $600 each and add that money to her coffers that was steadily growing.

Once Nikki left Lynn went to her computer and started to research stores that sold gift cards. She was excited to learn that gift cards could be loaded with $10-$500 and she planned to load them with the most money allowable. She was aware that they had been making so many returns to stores that they were beginning to be noticed.

Lynn thought about the time that a store rep actually asked her if she was there to make a return. She had replied no, but she actually was. That was a red flag for her to never return to that store again.

Lynn's trip down memory lane was interrupted by a call from Reggae.

"Hey love," Lynn said to her favorite little cousin.

"Girl I just got off the phone with Nikki. She is off the hook for running out of that store like that. Suppose y'all had gotten caught?"

"Yes and you know I was scared. This fat bitch come running out the store screaming for me to pull off. I was like what bitch?" Lynn was cracking up.

Reggae was her best worker and she could confide everything about Team Concrete to her. Reggae laughed uncontrollably.

"Well, she also told me about the gift card discovery. What's going on with that boo?"

"Oh she told you already damn. But I am online looking for them now. I've never paid them any attention until today."

"Right, me either. And you know me girl so I have already been thinking we can buy our own things and get the gift cards for you to sell that way we don't have to return things for store credit for you to sell."

"That's why you're my bitch. That's exactly the plan. But I would keep the electronics still."

"Yes, that makes sense," Reggae said, but she sighed. "You know someone is going to complain again like in Miami. We're getting things that we normally wouldn't and traveling so I don't think it's no big deal but she has just been making some little snide remarks."

"People can be a pain in the ass with their complaining. But as long as everyone plays their part, we are good. I am going to get all of this together and meet with everyone about this."

"Yo I am on my way over, 'cause here comes Renee and you know she can't hear me talking about this."

CHAPTER 16

Lynn sat back on her sofa reading an urban fiction novel, when the doorbell took her out of her fantasy world. She sat the book aside and then opened the front door, after she peeped out the window and saw Reggae's car.

"Girl, I need a new car ASAP," Reggae said and walked through the door looking like a true fashionista. She was already a fly girl, but the scam that she had been running had her really looking good. "That damn tramp did not want to turn over a minute ago," she yelled and fell on the sofa.

"Damn," Lynn said, and then added, "I understand. It's just about time that you get one. I was trying to wait for Christmas to be over so that I could save some cash to give you. It seems you may not be able to wait though."

"Hell no bitch. Get me a rental or something," she said and laughed. It wasn't a joking matter, but she had to make light of it to keep from crying.

Lynn chuckled and said "Matter of fact, let's rap right now and figure out how to do this gift card thing."

Reggae was Lynn's heart, and they've been close forever. Reggae was just her nick name because she loved that style of music. She loved to dance to it so much, which kept her body tight and fit.

"You know it only took me five minutes to come up with a plan, right?" Lynn expressed to Reggae with a smile on her face. She had begun to feel powerful in her new crafty position as boss.

Reggae laughed. "I bet it was three minutes."

"Probably, anyway like you said y'all can get the gift cards and keep your clothes or whatever else that you buy. I'll introduce my people to the gift cards and sell them for half the value."

"Do you think the money can be deleted off the cards available balance by the company if they find out before someone spends the money on them?" Reggae asked.

"Good question, but not my concern right now. What I can do is give my customers one day to get to the store after I sell them the card."

"I know that's right. I wanted to know because people are going to try to play you and beg you to give them a bigger deal than half."

"Well, right now it's so new and I'm not having anyone short change me. They will get half off basically. Real talk, its buy one get one free almost. I swear I have no issue cursing anyone out. Normally I just sell to Norman and Rico, and they don't give me issues. They always have my money right. Hell they even tip sometimes," Lynn said laughing.

"Oh, shit well you good."

77

"Yeah, I'm waiting to hear back from Tru, to see what she made at mall today."

"She went alone?" asked Reggae. She seemed concerned.

"Hell yea. She always does. She got that from me. It's better and quicker to hop store to store alone than having somebody with you and them asking for something, or another worker buying the same things. It's just safer to be alone."

"What's new though since we got that figured out?"

"Well I do have a surprise for y'all, and since you're here I'll tell you now."

"Surprise, okay" she said smiling. "I like the sound of that." She said walking towards the kitchen.

Lynn knew that was most likely to dig in the refrigerator.

"First road trip baby." Lynn screamed out of nowhere. That was the surprise.

"What? About time. Finally." Reggae yelled running back from the kitchen. Reggae had been asking for a road trip since we started.

"Yea I know. I think we can hit more states along the drive. Whereas flying is limited. I finally feel comfortable enough driving with the equipment also so we going to hit the Mall Of America in Minnesota baby."

"Bitch, that's the biggest mall in the US isn't it? OMG. Imagine the shoes." She started dancing around the living room.

It felt so good for Lynn to see her excitement. She could not wait to talk to the rest of the girls. Lynn sat back and just pondered, as Reggae snacked on a piece of cake. She thought about how wrong she was for hustling stores out of their merchandise and money, but that was why they had insurance.

She had a family to feed in the meantime, which extended beyond her little sister. She wanted to take care of her village and she tried hard to keep her mind off the negative fact that she robbed and stole from hard working people to do it.

Although this new lick was Lynn's first illegal hustle, she had been getting money since she was 14-years-old. She was fired and learned that nothing lasted forever. At 18-years-old she had gotten her first official at Boston's, a major department store located in downtown Chicago. She had started as a cashier, with a desire to sell women's shoes, but the store required employees to have prior experience. Her job at Boston's though, helped her tremendously with her new crime spree.

At Boston's Lynn was encouraged to get customers to open Boston charge cards. She passed that encouragement on to the customers and for everyone that did she memorized their card numbers. She loved the rich white women, because they were typically approved for $2,500. She would take their number and go to another area of the store and shop with it. She'd tell her fellow sales team that she didn't have the card, but knew the account number. They always let her get away with it too.

There was even a time that her godson needed a winter coat, and she had used one of her good account numbers to get it. She had called her job and ordered the coats to be picked up. She arrived at her job with her best friend; they picked up the coats and left the store. Loss prevention staff waited at the exit, and Lynn spoke to them as she walked out like she normally did.

The next day Lynn learned that she was not in the clear. She was at her register ringing up a customer and as soon as the man walked away Chicago PD kindly handcuffed her and walked her off the sales floor. She was arrested and felt stupid for foolishly having something picked up. She could have waited because she had a good thing going at the registers. Being thirsty had gotten her caught and with her new crime, she was taking it slow and easy.

Reggae finished her cake and they picked up the conversation like several minutes of silence had not passed.

"That's the second largest mall, by the way. It is smaller than King of Prussia Mall outside Philly, but it has over 120 more stores. It don't matter any way, I am just ready to do damage."

"Okay, looks like you've been doing your research."

"Yes, I have. We're leaving on Friday. It's a six hour trip, so I want to head out early."

Reggae stood, and said, "Let me get out of here to start packing."

"Pack? You're crazy. We're going to shop, so there's no need to pack, bitch. I am making us five cards each."

When Reggae left, Lynn settled down and prepared for a hot bath. The water ran, and she made a hotel reservation and reserved a SUV for her and the girls. That put her down $2,000 and she needed the girls to recoup that in Minnesota. John had dropped the price that Lynn paid for card numbers because she returned for more cards frequently. She was receiving 25 numbers for $1,500, and she appreciated the huge price drop, but it made her wonder how cheap he had gotten the numbers for.

What he had bought them for was a concern to her because she had heard that other people were doing the same thing as her and her team. People in the hood loved to gossip, and she had heard rumors about people being arrested for using false cards. At that point no one knew what she was doing, but she was learning from the rumors to school her team not to make the same mistakes. Chicago was getting hot and she was excited about going to the Mall of America and other places so that she can continue to make her money.

Breaking her thoughts once her sister came into her room. She picked up the printout with the hotel confirmation on it and asked, "So where are you going now?"

"I am going to the Mall of America to handle some business. It's just for two days, and I will certainly bring you some things back. I just need you to hold the house down and stay out of trouble while I am gone. Can you do that?"

"Yup I can, but when are you going to take me to handle some business. I know what's going, you know."

"I am sure that you do, but I want you to stay out of this. Let me make this money, and you'll never have to worry about anything, and definitely not committing a crime."

Janell fell onto Lynn's bed and said, "I want to do it so that I can get my own things and stack my own money."

"Girl, what the hell are you talking about? I give you money and I buy you everything that you need. You're not grown."

Janell sat there and looked at her sister with a frown. She understood, but she didn't want to hear it. "I guess, I'll be here when you get back," she said with an air of sarcasm.

"Just be patient, Janell. I need you to graduate and go to college. Get a good job and get the hell out of Chicago. If not I would have done all of this shit for nothing. Sure, I make money, but I do this to protect you from being shot like many of your friends and associates. That's why we live out here. Come on, don't break down on me, okay, sis."

Janell laid back and stared at the ceiling. She thought about her mom and just shook her head.

"Okay, Lynn. But while you're there can you bring me back some Burberry?"

Lynn smiled. "What the hell you know about Burberry?"

"Chile pahleeese. My friend, Raynesha mom went to that mall and bought her some printed Burberry skirts and shirts. I like that plaid. Can you please get me some?"

"I will see what I can do."

They both laughed.

Janell said, "I know you're going to do it," and burst into laughter. She couldn't help spoiling her baby sister.

CHAPTER 17

The next morning, Lynn and the girls barreled up I-90W in a rented Cadillac Escalade. They had the music blaring and jammed to the local R&B radio station. It was all smiles and joy, as they were embarking on the next phase of their sometimes lucrative business. There were days that they made a lot of money and on other days their plan was derailed by overzealous employees that looked to save the company from their thievery. But Minneapolis, Minnesota was a new ground for them and they were ready to leave a mark on it. Everyone took turns driving but Lynn would only fall asleep if Reggae was behind the wheel.

Lynn had laced the girls with 10 cards each and they were prepared to do the unthinkable. They wanted merchandise, gift cards and electronics. Money was all that they had on their minds and Lynn was proud that she had managed to keep the girls in a position to continue making money for her and her compadres.

They reached the Rockford area and Lynn saw a Wal-Mart and told her team, "Let's stop at this Wal-Mart and get some toiletries, hit the bathroom and snacks. We can also get gas on the way out."

She parked in the vast lot and watched the girls pile out of the truck. Lynn hustled them together, and said, "Get some gift cards while you're in there. Be extra cautious and do not all get into the same line.

We may as well make some money on this six hour drive."

"A very boring one might I add," Nikki said. They all laughed and headed into the store.

Thirty minutes later, they were all back in the parking lot and handed gift cards to Lynn.

"You know what, y'all keep them. We have bigger fish to fry."

Tru placed the cards in her back pocket and said, "You ain't gotta tell me twice." Everyone laughed.

"You're too much Hun," Lynn said to Tru. "Nikki, can you drive. You drive the fastest. Although, I gotta keep one eye open with you."

*   *   *

Six hours later, the girls were in downtown St. Paul and checked into the Riverfront Crowne Plaza hotel. They all went into their rooms and freshened up a bit before they all met in the lobby to head to the mall. In less than an hour they were back in the car and headed to make money. That was their reason for visiting the city, and not to play games.
About a half hour after leaving the hotel, the ladies pulled into the parking lot of the Mall of America. They were excited and very talkative.

"Damn, do y'all see this shit?" Nikki yelled. The truck windows were down so she caught stares from some people walking pass. She stared right back, held her head out of the window and said, "It's my first time here. What the fuck y'all staring for?"

The entire crowd burst into laughter. Nikki was always a ball of comedy with her antics.

Through laughter, Tru said, "G chill yo crazy ass out. You slow as hell." They continued to laugh at the loony bin.

Lynn broke all that up and said, "Y'all just do what you have to do and be safe in this mall." It was a warning.

"We're parked in section B23, and I am leaving the truck doors unlocked so that you all will have access to drop off bags and chill to smoke if you have to."

After all of the woman chit chatted, they all dispersed into the mall. Tru and Lynn stayed back to talk for a moment.

"Sis, this bitch is huge. Look at the damn roller coaster. This is nuts," Tru said as they walked slowly into the mall. She didn't seem up for the job at hand.

Lynn chuckled, and asked, "Why do you insist on calling me sis when we are cousins fool?"

"You know I get that from Viv. I just wanted to make sure that we were cool."

"We are fine, Hun. I am no longer pissed, but please when you're done working you check in. We have to be on point with that. I was very worried when you didn't reply to my text about being done. This is like a job. You check in with me when you start and check out when you're done. I just want us all safe." Lynn told her sincerely.

"I got you, and I am sorry. Don't be mad at me."

"I'm not. Now let's get to shopping, sis," Lynn said and smiled.

*   *   *

After spending three days in the mall, Lynn was at the lobby bar of the Crowne Plaza having a stiff drink the night before they were scheduled to check out. The weekend intake at the mall was huge, and she had to drink a little just to realize what had happened in The North Star State.

In the three days they had collectively her team had gotten her $22,000 in gift cards. *Too bad that I can't pay my bills with these cards*, she thought and was fine with that. She'd earn at least $11,000 from the gift cards, and was not taking any shorts from the buyers. *I need all my money.* She had no idea how much they had spent on them, but by the looks of the bags they had spent nearly $70,000. They had bought so much that they had to ship things home each day because the poor truck was filled with merchandise.

Lynn had become so spoiled that she had no desire to pay for McDonald's with cash. It was sad, but why should she waste cash on food, when she had cards.

Lynn was tapped on her shoulder, and spun around ready for war. For all she knew it was a police officer.

"I don't know about you," Tru said, and waved at the bartender. "But I am ready for the next city."

"And so am I," Lynn said and smiled. "I am going to look into that."

CHAPTER 18

A few months later, Lynn was sitting in her truck as three men waxed the tires.

She was doing some planning when her cell phone rang. It was John who had been making life very easy for her. For the past two months, she had been giving him alot of cash at a time for numbers and he was feeling good about that. Her deal with him had become better and better.

She answered the phone, and he said, "Mamacita, I need you to go meet my boy and do his stuff. I am in a rush to get to O'Hare for a vacation."

Lynn furrowed her brow and looked around puzzled.
"Are you sure? You never wanted me to meet anyone." She was shocked because he was a very paranoid man and it aggravated her at times. Once, he had talked to her next to a running tow truck just in case she wore a wire. John had been arrested in the past after being set up and he didn't want that to happen again.

"Yeah. Yeah. He's cool. I just gotta get out of town before my wife kills me. With the way you roll we are sitting pretty," John said.
I bet you're, she thought then said, "Alright text me his info."

"Thanks, I am going to E-mail you some numbers for doing this. Thanks."

"Free?" She asked, and chuckled. "I'll take care of more things for you," she said. It was a serious joke that she would consider.

"Yes this time. You know that I do not usually do this, but I have to get my wife out of town so that she can stop complaining that I don't take her anywhere. The text is coming and be careful. Blue is a big flirt, so be ready. He will pounce on you."

*   *   *

Blue was parked on Michigan Avenue and 113th Street in front of a City Sports clothing store. When he saw Lynn pull up, he stepped out of his car and walked over to her. A loud CTA bus rolled pass them and they remained silent until it was out of the way.

"Nice to finally meet you," Blue said and smiled. He held out his hand and said, "I've heard so much about how beautiful you were, but now I know."

"Thanks," Lynn replied shaking his hand. "So what can I do for you?" she asked as she slyly checked out his smooth dark complexion.

Blue ran his hand along his mustache and then said, "I can think of a few things that you can do. They involve a bedroom though." He smiled until he saw the wicked smile on Lynn's face.

"Let me be frank. I'm trying to fuck a dollar, not a dick," she said and let that sink in. "You got that?"

He nodded his head and raised his eyebrows. He hadn't heard a woman be so raunchy in quite a long time. He chuckled, but her forwardness has shocked him.

"Now that you're aware that there is a woman in Chicago that's not falling for your game, let's get to business. How many cards do you need written?"

"Twenty-five. Something small to a giant like you."

"Twenty-five," she said loudly, and then cupped her hands over her mouth. In a lower tone, she said, "John only said a few."

"I know, Lil Mama but please calm down," he said with his hands in the air. He grinned, and handed her a jump drive. "There are two files on there. The one named John has five numbers on it that he wanted done. The other file is from another connect of his."

"What nigga? I am not doing that shit for free. I don't know you like that, plus no one is doing this but John," she told him matter of factly with her hands on her hips.

"Girl ha, your first mistake is thinking that you're in some exclusive club. John ain't the only nigga rocking on the card side. The proof is in your hands. I was going to pay you $10 a card for a total payout of $250, but I'mma do you one better. Take both files and use them for yourself and let me know if they were better than John's."

Lynn's spot to make the cards were nearby, and she had no intentions of letting him know where she did her business. "I'll be right back."
"I'll be right here waiting."

*   *   *

Lynn pulled off and her cell phone immediately rang. She looked at the caller ID. It was Viv. *Now what the hell does she want now with her begging butt?* Lynn answered and simply asked,

"What's up?"

Viv, as expected, asked for money to buy concert tickets and an outfit to wear. Not just for her, but her friends too.

"Look honey, I can't keep spoiling your butt. Not only do you want something, but you're asking for your friends too? I am not made of money," Lynn replied and playfully scolded her. Once again she was begging and Lynn could not tell her no. But this time she wants money for her and two friends and that was too much. "Hell, no. I can't do that."

"Please sis? Matter of fact, I'll pay for myself but please help my friends. They don't have much and I want to help them."
Lynn understood that. That was the reason that she gave a lot of things away - to help people.

"I have a better idea. My place is in shambles, because I have been running around and traveling a lot. If they're not thieves, you all can work for the tickets. Yo ass probably want front row tickets too, so clean clean clean."

Lynn doubted she would go for working for the money.

"Oh, you know I love to clean, especially if I am getting paid," Viv said and seemed very excited.

"I am ready when you are. Just come get us. Thanks."

*   *   *

Back at the house, Lynn inserted the jump drive into the computer prepared to make the cards for Blue. The file titled "John" took no time to load up and download onto the cards. The second file was labeled "Hot Shit" and it took a while to open. She noticed something called Track 1 and Track 2.

That confused her because she had never seen that and she had questions for Blue. She gathered the cards and jump drive and tossed them into an envelope and raced back out to meet Blue.

When she was back in Blue's presence, she smiled as he walked over to her car. Something about him makes me feel comfortable; looking like the singer Tyrese. He's cocky, but it's sexy to me. I ain't trying to have sex with him, though but I am going to use my looks to my advantage for the additional information. He had some pretty girl in the front seat of his car and Lynn wondered if he had just met her as she passed him.

Blue hopped into the passenger seat of Lynn's car and she handed him the envelope with his cards.

"Good luck ma," he said, and reached for the door handle.

"Damn, you jetting awfully quick!"

"Yeah, I got Shorty in the car and she ready to hit the streets. I know that you noticed that the work was in a woman's name?"

"Okay, I won't hold you, but what's up with the two different tracks?"

He chuckled. "You noticed, huh? Here's the deal, track one will let you go anywhere. I know you have been to JC Penney or Sears and sometimes the cards won't get read by the machine."

"Yes, that has happened and me and my team don't go to several stores, because we know they don't go for the lick."

"Oh, but they do, ma. See the register be reading both tracks. More than likely you never clean your cards so track one is different than track two. That throws the computer off. If I was you be sure to ask John for the track one numbers. He may charge you more, but once you see the additional stores that you can hit, the money won't matter."

Lynn was steaming with anger. "Why the hell he ain't been telling me that?"

"I don't know. He be on some extra shit. That's why I keep more than one connect. On that note, I'm out. Let me know what he charges you because you owe me for that good downtown shopping that you're about to do." He stepped out the car and closed the door.

"Yeah, whatever, nigga. You just tricked without a treat."She laughed and skidded off into traffic. She immediately called John and gave him an earful. She demanded the track one numbers and she assured him that she was not paying any extra because it should be included. The way she saw it, if there were more stores to hit she'd make more money, which would make him more and faster.

Chapter 19

A day later, Lynn was on the magical and fashion forward Magnificent Mile. She walked to the front of the Coach store and breathed in deeply. She was alone and had not told any of the girls about her mission because she didn't want them in the downtown area. She needed them to stay modest and humble. She feared that designer labels would corrupt them. There was a bit of arrogance that came with wearing Prada and Gucci and she wanted to keep them away from that.

"Welcome to Coach," the door greeter said to her, as he held the door for her.

"Thank you," she said and smiled at him. *Such a professional and pleasant atmosphere* she thought and watched a customer being offered champagne.

She was immediately accosted by a quirky salesman that looked like a college student. He smiled and asked to help her with a little giggle. He was just a happy youngman.

"My best friend is pregnant with my God baby, and I'd love to get her that baby carrying bag," Lynn said and nodded towards the shelf with the bag.

"Oh, that's a beautiful idea," he said, and grabbed it for her. He put it in her hands and said, "For $409 that's a steal."

Normally a $409 purchase was a no go for Lynn, but this spree was on someone else. She continued to look around at all of the shoes and bags and fell in love.

She was not a fan of Louis Vuitton or Gucci because everyone had fake versions of it, and people always asked was the pieces real. She had the rep grab her three hobo bags and matching shoes.

Ohhhh, wait until I see Tru, she thought. They were not really up on the downtown designers, because Lynn had forbid them from going down there. The salesman rang her up and the total was $1878 and she wanted to clutch her pearls. She nervously pulled out her card, because she did not like downtown shopping at all. Especially after her Nordstrom arrest. She knew how advanced their security was and she did not want to get arrested for being greedy.

"Would that be cash, check or charge?"

"I wouldn't have that much cash and checks are so outdated. Let's see if this Visa will work?" She asked and handed him the card.

"Cross your fingers," she said and giggled.

The salesman actually crossed his fingers, and smiled at her. He swiped the card, and didn't even glance at the name or signature panel before handing it back to her. She tucked it back into her wallet as the receipt came spitting out of the register. He bagged her things and then handed her two large shopping bags. Done!

Beat!
Before she spun to leave, she asked, "Oh, I almost forgot, do you sell gift cards?"

"Absolutely."

"Great, I need two for $500 each."

CHAPTER 20

Lynn drove to her best friend's Zoe home and pondered about what had been happening over the past few months. After the trip to the Mall of America, the crew were hooked on traveling. Since that time they had been to Ohio, Missouri, and Tennessee. Hollywood was her favorite. It smelled of old long money. And that was Lynn's long term goal. To stack some long, long money. Every weekend they were away somewhere getting money. Lynn didn't know about the other girls, but she was staking money. She had it hidden in a few of her trustworthy older friend's homes. She had been selling more cards to people who had an excuse to need more money or some help. It was easier to do that than to keep giving people money.

For the upcoming weekend they were planning to fly to Orlando, Florida. They didn't want to take any more road trips because they took too long and they would fall asleep. Lynn remembered during a car ride to Kentucky that she had dozed off and when the tires hit the rubble the whole van was shook up. It scared everyone awake and it was safe to assume no one wanted to chance driving more than 6 hours again. Jumping because the ringing of her Samsung scared her. The caller ID said unknown.

"Yo!" I yelled at the caller.

"Hey L, how you doing? This Taylor," she said like I knew her.

"Ok..." I replied puzzled. "What's up?"

"I hope I didn't catch you at a bad time, but my uncle Kris said you always sell him gift cards and I wanted to know if you needed any extra hands?" Taylor said timidly.

Blown away was the only word I could use to describe my feelings. People out here talking? Why the fuck would Kris give anyone my number. It's over for his ass. But I'm not gonna take it out on her.

"What can you do?" I asked her.

"Well I used to work at target and I'm aware of how c.cs work. When I was on the register, I would have my friends come in there and hand me a card with fake numbers written down on a taped piece of paper.."

I started laughing so hard.

"I know it sounds dumb but we were good for about two months before they installed a camera system that could zoom down on us and we can't punch the numbers in any longer. I got 3 babies and the holidays are coming soon." She was tearing up. I hate a sad story.

"Wow I was laughing because I've done that before at Kmart. Haha, I thought that was risky but hey we gotta eat don't we?"

"I'm not gonna lie and say I'm not going to curse Kris ass out, but I respect that you're trying to grind. Right now though it's so much on my plate, I can't meet up and get you together just yet, but it's definitely on my mind. Gimme til after Xmas and I'll get you straight. Until then I'll have my cousin meet you and give you a gift card to Walmart for your babies." I told her.

"Lord thank you! wow, I wasn't expecting that. I've heard good things about you too. You stay helping people. I appreciate you so much and look forward to being down if you let me. Have a great Halloween, Thanksgiving and Xmas!!" She said happily.

"You too. No problem, bye bye!"

* * *

Lynn pulled up to Zoe's and couldn't believe how long it had been since she had last seen her. Zoe was a white acting girl trapped in a black body that had went to the army after their high school. She had a banging body and was far from prissy or dumb. Today she was Zoe, and tomorrow she'd be Dakota or Madison. She was a proper speaking woman, but loved to name herself after cities and states. Lynn would call her, Zoe and she'd reply: "This is Carolina." Lynn would crack up in laughter. She loved fitness and only ate fish and turkey, which made her look perfect.

Zoe's condo was on the east side by the lake. She could not be paid to live west of Cottage Grove. Lynn approached the security of Zoe's building and was let right up because he knew her face. Lynn smiled entering the elevator because it moved so fast and reminded her of being on a roller coaster.

"Best friend, how you been?" Zoe asked while swinging her door open.

"Hey, Zoe, I've been well. Missing ya ass, so here take my coat," Lynn said and handed her a fall jacket.
"Let's chat, boo, I know you have some things to tell me." Lynn loved to hear Zoe stories. She was single without children like Lynn and the crew. Zoe flew through men like she flew country to country in the army.

"No hoe, let's get started on you first. From all of your myspace posts you've been extra happy and fly as hell. I can smell a lick somewhere," she said and sniffed in the air.
She looked hard at Lynn and dared her to lie about it.
I forgot this bitch knows me, Lynn thought. Zoe and

Lynn went back to ninth grade. She knew that Lynn was a hustler more than anyone. In high school, Lynn and her other best friend Kissa sold candy bags, candy bars, sandwiches and sunglasses to other students. Lynn always held a job since the age of 14. Later in college, Kissa and Lynn used to steal credit card numbers and order things from Wal-Mart and other retailers. Lynn thought, a legal job was cool, but she believed that one must hustle to live comfortably.

"Well, honey since you're so nosey. Me and my little crew have been beating the pavement basically. I got a certified card hook up that gives me stolen credit card numbers to put on pre-paid cards."Lynn said.

"I've been stacking," Lynn said and then filled Zoe in on the entire scam. "We're going to Orlando next."

"Girl, are you serious. Free shopping?"
"Well, not free. I pay for the numbers from my connect and we risk our freedom. It definitely ain't free, Hun."

"Yo, butt know what I mean," Zoë said and smiled. "Damn bitch put me down. I want to go to Orlando also."

"What about your army duties?"

"Girl, I'm on reserve now. So, I just do one weekend a month unless I get deployed. So, other than that monthly check I'm unemployed."

It wasn't even much to think about, but Lynn needed to make a quick decision. And she did. Her friend asked and she was obliging. That was what friends did. *When one eat; we all eat,* Lynn thought.

"Are you sure you want to get involved with this, Zoe? It's very addictive. Good thing is that you're coming in at a good time. I am about to let them all go to do their own thing. It's about time to distance myself from the group and just do my own thing."

"Look, hell yeah, I am sure. I don't need the cash like that. I just need the merchandise."

"Okay, that's cool," Lynn said. She was excited about having one of her best friends on her team.
"I am going to let them know that after this Orlando trip, I am putting them on to the connect and they can do them. Things are good now, but you know how I feel about happiness."

"Yeah, if it's too much happiness going on, something bad is bound to be lurking around the corner." Zoe had recited Lynn's line about fear with ease. She had lived by that with all of her flames all over the world.

"I just can't ever shake my fear of happiness. Some shit bad always happens to balance out the happiness."

"True that, so what's good with everyone? I know you have been having drama with all of them females!"

Lynn needed to get a little more comfortable to really catch up with her best friend. She went into the kitchen and grabbed a Pepsi. "I am surprised you have Pepsi in here."

"That's some dude's pop."

"Oh, I am sorry," Lynn said headed back to the kitchen.

"Drink that shit. I told him not to leave his shit at my house. Don't even use my garbage. Niggas think they're slick like bitches. Plus, Pepsi is to damn tempting. It's liquid crack. One swallow and you're hooked."
Lynn spit her pop out from bursting out in laughter.

"You're still crazy as hell. I can't wait to put you on to this lick. So far I have not had any issues. Reggae ain't with the drama; you know that. She's fearless and right now bringing in the most money. Tru and Nikki are a mess. They keep our road trips funny with all of their bickering. Nikki ass had to run outta Foot Locker. It was a funny sight to see."

For a few hours Lynn and Zoe exchanged stories and drank Pepsi's just like the good old days. They capped off with Lynn promising to take her shopping the next day to show her how the game works.

*   *   *

The next day, Zoe and Lynn went shopping at the Water Tower Place Mall. Lynn had planned to do the shopping, but Zoe insisted on getting her feet wet. Lynn accompanied Zoe to the first few stores and then let her run through the mall all alone. They split up and both set out to get some things that they needed.

Two hours later, Zoe met Lynn at the car and had some man carrying some of her bags. She had that many.

"Girl, I literally maxed out all of my cards," she said as she approached Lynn. "Taught my husband about cheating on me," she added and smiled at the man helping her. She told him, "Thanks for your help. I hope you're not a cheater?"

"No ma'am," he said and smiled back her. "Good luck with your marriage," he said and then turned to walked back into the mall.

"Chile, I had to get help with these bags and I told him that I was maxing out my husband's credit cards for cheating."

"Well, I guess he brought it," Lynn said opening the car trunk.

"And I bought you these," Zoë said and fanned out twelve gift cards. "I know you told me to get what I wanted without paying you, but you're a business woman and I can't knock that."

Lynn gave her a hug, and said, "See, this is why you're my bitch. How much is here?"

"It's $1,800."

"You've made me very happy, boo. It's good to know what kind of person you are," Lynn said, and then handed her friend some cards back.

"Let's split this. I like your style."

"Thanks, girl. Now let's the hell from downtown."

"Absolutely."

CHAPTER 21

Friday morning the team piled into Lynn's living room for what they thought was a chance to catch up without working. Lynn planned to surprise them with the trip out of town to get busy.

Reggae, Tru and Nikki was asking about the limo parked in front of Lynn's door when the doorbell rang. After the bell there was a hard incessant knock at the door.

Where the hell are these dumbasses running to? Lynn thought as Nikki and Tru ran towards the bedrooms like it was the police. Lynn knew it wasn't, but she envisioned that it could be and shook her head.

Lynn opened the door and when Reggae saw who was standing there she started yelling and jumping up and down. Nikki and Tru came out of hiding, as if the cops wouldn't have searched the whole house, they screamed too.

"Zoe," they all sang with excitement.

They all nearly knocked Lynn down to shower Zoe with hugs and kisses. They had no clue that she was in town and was shocked to see her. She was like family to them, too. They knew her well because she had lived with Lynn because she didn't get along with her own mother. Although, Lynn's mother was an alcoholic, she was the best mother one could ask for. Lynn's aunt Tiff preached that Lynn's father Dwayne had ran Lynn's mother to drinking because of his womanizing ways. He had five daughters in total, all younger than Lynn, and not by her mother. It was because of that Lynn was in no rush to have children.

"Look at those abs and when did you get back?" Reggae asked touching Zoe's firm stomach.

They all sat around the dining room table and bombarded Zoe with questions, while Lynn slipped outside. She informed the limo driver that they'd be ready in an hour. Their flight left at 1 p.m. and it was only 9 a.m.

When Lynn stepped back in, Tru asked Lynn was Zoe the reason she had them all there.

"Nope, she's joining the team."

"Oh shit," Tru said and stood up. "Attention, bitches," Tru said and started laughing. She always made jokes about Zoe's military experience.

"Another addition to the team. About time," Nikki said. She looked adorable in a lime green Adidas jogging suit with the Classics to match.

"Yes, I am down bitches. There's a new sergeant in town," she said jokingly. "Now let's catch this flight."

"Flight?"The girls asked in unison.

"You got it. That limo outside is about to take us to O'Hare. We're out of here, and before you ask no bags needed this time either. We can buy shit there," Lynn said and simply smiled.

*   *   *

At the airport all of the girls were jealous of Zoe, because she used her military ID to head through the First Class TSA line. When the all met up at the gate, Tru had pulled Lynn to the side and confided in her that she had successfully gotten weed through airport security.

Lynn was pissed. She replied, "I don't know what the fuck it is with you weed smokers, but why the hell would you risk your freedom for a two hour high. That was dumb as shit." She was starting to think that flying was a bad idea. Every airport trip they had a situation.

Tru stopped laughing and couldn't believe how harsh Lynn was. She didn't reply and just waited for the flight clerk to announce boarding on the flight. Lynn and Tru were sat next to each other on the plane. They both had the screw face.

When the plane taxied, Tru looked over at Lynn and said, "Watchu mad for, bitch? I was going to jail not you."

"I don't give a damn. You jeopardized this whole team and could have drawn attention on us. That's selfish and fucked up. If you can't think about the safety of all of us, then perhaps you don't need to be here. And before you get all mad, know that I am pissed that I could have gotten arrested fucking with you, because I have the card making material in my bag."

Tru sat there for a moment, and then apologized. "You made a lot of sense. Just forgive me."

Despite how upset Lynn was she let it go. "I don't even want to sit next to your ass," Lynn said and frowned. She then chuckled, and said, "But I have to be here and so do you. Let's make the best out of it."And on that note the rest of the flight to Florida was smooth sailing.

CHAPTER 22

Orlando, Florida was a beautiful state and the palm trees looked refreshing. It had a more serene feeling than Miami. There was a light wind and the air smelled much different than the polluted Chicago air.

The girls were at the Hertz car rental checkout counter and they chose a nondescript Dodge Caravan. It was much better than a Cadillac Escalade or Yukon Denali because it wouldn't be as flashy and make them targets for police contact.

Lynn had gotten a two bedroom suite at the Marriott Residence Inn hotel. The hotel was at the airport because after careful research, Lynn learned that the airport was accessible to all of the roads that would get them in and out of the malls quickly. She only reserved one room because she loved how the girl cracked jokes and bonded in the room. One of her main goals was to teach the girls how to love and respect people.

Zoe wanted to hit the pool with the girls so they all got changed and talked shit.

"Nikki, you losing weight or something?" Reggae asked when Nikki walked confidently out of the bathroom in a two piece suit.

"You think so?" Nikki asked. She grinned hard at the compliment. "I got a little boo, so I am trying to get this body right. I've been working out, too."

All of the ladies clapped their hands, because she definitely needed a man to get some sexual healing.

"That good dick must have given you an attitude adjustment," Lynn said.

"Yes, you have been nicer," Reggae said and laughed.

"Don't let dude stop your paper," Zoë said, and winked. "Hoes fall in love and the money falls right with 'em."

"Oh, you see that I am here. I ain't with that. As the saying goes, money over bitches."

They all burst into laughter again and then headed to the pool. Everybody discussed their favorite brands and stores. "Im so happy I can fit Victoria Secret, thank you universe!" Nikki crazy self shouted.

"Yes baby. Macy's has the best shoe section," Tru agreed.

This is the life, everyone thought. While lounging around the pool laughing at the girls Lynn's cell phone rang.

"Ugh, why didn't I leave you upstairs?" She asked the phone, but after seeing a blocked number she was happy because mommy was on the line.

Smiling like she could see her Lynn giddily said "Hi mommy." "Hey baby, how is everyone, where

is my Nell Nell?" My mommy asked. She made sure
to ask about her favorite kid.

*   *   *

The next morning Zoe walked out of a Prada store in
the outlet mall and bumped into Lynn.

"Damn, bitch," Lynn said and tapped her
friends shoulder. "You have torn this outlet a new
asshole."

Zoe took a deep breath, and said, "Look, I am
out here trying to get my clothing closets like Kim K.
You got that? In the process, I am making my bestie
money." She handed Lynn ten gift cards in rubber
bands.

"They all have $1,000 each on them. That's
ten G's. Now if you don't mind that Anne Klein store
has my name on it."

Lynn was speechless as Zoe walked away. They
were on their third mall in the area, and Zoe seemed
to be the missing link. The team had only been in the
outlet mall an hour and Zoe had so many bags that
Lynn didn't think she'd be able to carry them all. I
guess the working out in the military gave Zoe strong
arms to carry the world on her shoulders. Lynn loved
every minute of it.

CHAPTER 23

After a fantastic and profitable weekend in Orlando, Lynn walked into her home and it was spotless. Viv and her friends had done a great job, and Lynn looked forward to sending them to the concert. She had a seat on the sofa and did a visual scan of the room for all of her belongings. She called Viv and told her that she had two Victoria's Secret jogging suits and a pair of Coach Sneakers. What she didn't tell her was that she also was giving her a Macy's gift card with $1,000 on it so that her and her friends could get clothing for the concert.

While Lynn waited for Viv, she prepared herself to sell the cards. She had several people lined up to buy gift cards, and was counting the money in her head. Lynn went to run a bath and turn on her CD player, expecting to hear her Scud Gang CD play. It didn't, so she hit the eject button on the player and the tray was empty. Scud Gang was a hot Chicago group from the projects that she had grew up in, and was steamed that it wasn't there. She heard the doorbell, and walked hastily to the door.
"Where the fuck is my CD?" Lynn said to Viv as she opened the door.

Viv pointed to her red haired girlfriend who shrugged her shoulders and looked at her feet. Lynn cleared her throat, and waited for a reply before she went crazy on both of them.

"I am sorry. Here are your CD's. I took them home to burn them. I know the Scud Gang and that

CD was rocking as we cleaned up. I just had to have it." The girl waved her hands and talked fast. "I wasn't stealing them."

"Who are you to bring your ass in my house and steal? Then return it. If you know the group support them and buy a CD, rather than bootlegging it. We all know them around here, you ain't special." Lynn backed into the house and crossed her arms as she stared hard at Viv.

"Sis, this is my friend Fancy," Viv said while pulling on Fancy's arm. "She and cousin Sky helped me clean up."

"Sky? You had her crazy ass out of the house?" Lynn was surprised to hear that she had come over.

"Yes, we're all going to the concert. But, Fancy did tell me that she had the CD." Viv explained.

Lynn bit her bottom lip and prayed that she did not choke the life out of both of them. She disliked people that stole from people that they knew. She only condoned stealing from corporations. This bitch brought this crazy ass child over here to rob me.

"Where is my Young Staks CD? There are two missing."
"Oh, that is stuck in the back of the player. I didn't take it, but dude Brandon spits hard. I went home and followed him on Facebook," Fancy said and pissed Lynn off more.

"Well, thanks for telling me. I haven't even listened to it yet," Lynn said and huffed. She was amped and ready to kill.

"Look, we have to rep Chicago hard, so stop stealing CDs and buy them."

"Thanks for understanding, and I am really sorry."
Lynn felt a good vibe from her but she had too much pride to act nice right away.

"Sis me and a few of my buddies went to volunteer at a women's shelter the other day, and it was so sad. I think we need to put something together to feed the homeless." Viv said sadly. That's why I loved her because she had a heart of pure gold.

"Now I'll definitely help you out with that. It's a great idea and you deserve all the blessings in the world for it!"

She smiled and said "I learn from the best."

CHAPTER 24

Nancy and Brian's Thanksgiving time cookout brought the who's who back to the Newtown area of Chicago. It's where one of the most popular projects was before the city tore it down and scattered everyone around the city. Nancy and Brian had been a couple for years, but refused to get married. Every year they threw a bash, and that year they had DJ Monty along with $5 shots.

Lynn and the girls all wore jeans or jogging suits since they were not going to a fancy club. Tru never missed an event and was there with Viv when Lynn arrived. Lynn had on warm fall colors with a light jacket. Surprisingly, it was nice outside, and no one complained. She hugged her girls Reggae, Renee and Fancy. Renee had her two friends, Whitney and May, with her. Nikki was nowhere in sight. *Late as usual,* Lynn thought.

"Just the two niggas I'm looking for," Lynn said to two men, Shug and Big Boy.

"Fuck yo thick ass want?"Big Boy said and added a devilish laugh.

He knew what she wanted, and Lynn looked at him crazily.

"Man, pay her ass before she acts up and shuts the party down," Shug said. "You know she don't play about her paper.

Both men were Lynn's brother Funnyman homies. No matter when or where they showed her love and looked out. They had asked her to get the liquor for the party. She did, and it was time to pay up.

"I don't so gimme my $600. You cheap ass niggas got all that money and still want a discount. I hate doing stuff for y'all," she said through laughter.

She was playing and talking shit to them like she always did. "Congrats on the engagement too. Bout time you stepping up to the plate instead of eating it. Now I'm not sure how lucky Miche is but at least you provide for them kids. Unless u eating they food too, fat ass!"

Big Boy walked away laughing, because he never talked smack for long. Shug could go all night, but Lynn had no time for that and wanted her money. He handed her the money, and she promised to take some pics with his fat ass later that evening. He shot a sexual advance at her and she promised to tell his fiancé and that shut him right up. She knew that he simply joked around, but all she needed was some nosey bitch to over hear their banter and misread it.

Lynn knew his fiancé, Mo and would never disrespect her by having sex with her man.
Lynn eventually made her way around the party and hugged her two pals, Lisa and Daisy. They were sisters.

"Lynn, what's good with the gift cards?" Daisy asked.

119

"Do you need any more workers? Lisa chimed in.

I started laughing and told them, "I work for self huns."

What all did they know I wondered.

Daisy had caught Lynn off guard, but she wasn't surprised by the question. Since she started helping people and sometimes giving away cards, she had everyone asking her for cards.

Even little kids were asking her for cell phones and dolls. *Who the fuck discussed crime around their children,* Lynn thought, and was glad that none of them had kids.

By the end of the night, Lynn had spent more time selling cards than dancing the night away as planned. Aside from having to stop Tru from almost slapping some girl for looking at her funny, the night went great. She loved to dance her ass off at parties, but that night she worked and had little fun.

Everyone wanted to prepare for Black Friday and she was fine with that. Hell, she had a great Black Thursday.

*   *   *

"Look at this bitch," Agent Jackson said to her partner. They were parked across the street from the party in a tinted Dodge Caravan.

"Yes she swears that she's the shit, but before she had them cards no one paid her ass any attention. The Ugg boots she has on may not even be real," Agent Dixon said as they both laughed. The agents had an air of jealousy in their assessments.

"I can't stand her or them hoes that she be with. They think they're fuckin' cute. I can't wait to get handcuffs on them. We just need a direct link to really prove what's going on."

"Yes, and look who it is at 2 a.m. and very fashionably late? Nikki. That's the one that we need to arrest and turn her against Lynn the ring leader."

The Next Day

"Damn Boss what's been up?" My bestie Tiana & Ciara said entering my living room after I opened the door.

I knew this pop up was coming soon.
Tiana has been my bff since 10th grade. We're often called peanut butter and jelly because I'm light skin and she's brown and were both thick. Tiana kids are my god son's.

Ciara is my ride or die. We met in high school but became closer after graduation. She's often mistaken for my sister because we look alike.

"Forgive me please. It's been busy, but I'm prepared with gifts." I said, giving them my best puppy dog expression. I walked over the mantle and picked up two pretty wrapped big boxes.

I need my besties to stay sane. They don't swipe and I'm grateful they don't want too. We don't talk much due to my busyness but as long as I know they got my back, I'm good.

"Gifts ya ass!" Ciara smart mouth ass replied. "If it aint no purse, I'm not forgiving shit." She pouted.

"Ok, well hell, if it aint some shoes, I aint forgiving either!" Tiana said with a smirk.

"Well you hoes came empty handed but mouths full. Shut the fuck up and open ya shits!" I yelled back at them laughing.

Now boths of their mouths are hanging over in shock. Tiana got her favorite, all purple everything. The new Coach Monogrammed sneakers with the matching bag. The Coach Watch and keychain. Ciara got the exact same thing but in Michael Kors and the colors were all White.
"Uh Huh-Whatcha say now?" I asked their asses cupping my ear. "I don't hear shit!" I was instantly flooded with hugs and kisses.

"Thank you bitch!"

"Thankssssss soo much!!"

I kept quiet that inside the new bags were gift cards to Macys and Children's place for my god kids.

They'll discover them whenever they wear the bags. I wasn't worried about the gift cards going off because I paid cash for them both. $500 each. They were my best friends, so the money meant nothing. Money doesn't have a value until you spend it anyway.

That night was a hard one for Lynn in particular because she knew if she went thru with her plans things would forever be different. None of the girls knew she knew about the lies and deceit. But Lynn was smart enough to know that this came with the game.

Her life has already been turned upside down and now she has doubts about doing it to them. Even though they'd love it, she knew it all came with a price.

Chapter 25

No one could believe Xmas was fast approaching. Black Friday seemed like it was just yesterday. It was a great Friday might I add. Every customer I had was happy. They all saved money with the gift cards and I even sent a few big money spenders some gas cards inside their Christmas cards.

All of the girls showed their asses too. It helped make my decision easier to allow everyone to work for themselves and build their own crew. After some long hard thinking I decided to let Viv and Renee in also.

They have 5 months to graduate and both are on the honor roll so I decided to let them shop especially since Renee has been shopping by accident. A few weeks ago I decided to do Reggae cards for her since she was busy one day.

After counting her cards and shifting thru them I noticed Renee had cards with her name on them. That means Reggae had been put her on and had her working. I was livid and hurt but decided to stay quiet.

I know you may think I'm dumb but I figured I trust Reggae and times may really be hard. So if she had to betray me then she may have had a good reason. I never confronted her about it but I decided to let Viv in as well. They all will get a welcome package on Christmas.

"Who's helping clean?" yelled a very intoxicated Tru. Later that evening after a house full and gifting everyone Lynn was tired and hoped to never have to have Christmas as her house again. Sleepy but tired Lynn was determined to give the girls the best gift of the night.

After all the cleaning was finished the girls all gathered in the living room, some sitting on the floor pillows. Viv and Renee were there as well.

"Well gals the time has come." I said.

"Time for what? Bitch I know you aren't putting us out this late?" Tru's crazy ass replied.

I just rolled my eyes and began speaking.

"It time for yall to branch off. I think it's time for everyone to just buy from me and work for themselves. Viv will be taught what to do and Renee has already been working without my permission so she knows the game." I stated finally looking at Reggae.

She put her head down in shame but I let it go.

Everyone will get the same deal. 25 cards for $750. I'll do them for you as long as you tell me ahead of time.

There will be no replacements. Your 25 cards should work, they all may not but you are guaranteed to at least flip your $750."

They all sat their looking shocked, "I think it's only fair everyone gets a chance to save some money.

We all have enough clothes and material shit. Now this is a chance for you guys to stack, if you haven't already found a way to do so."

"Can we have others working for us?" Asked Renee. This was the question I feared, everyone is not fit to lead. You can or should definitely be able to take care of yourself. But leading a team is only for a chosen few.

"Honestly that's up to you. The extra money would be good but I can already see the headache. Loyalty is hard to find and greed is at every corner. I say stack some cash in case you have to pay for their mistakes!" I stressed.

"A bit of advice. That cashier is your best friend until you're out the door. Black girls hate, gay guys know the deal and regular guys don't care. So that leaves them and the slow old white ladies! Be careful, no gift card is worth your freedom. Another Day-Another Dollar!" They all yelled together.

Nicki who was quiet the whole time finally spoke up.
"Damn yall," she started tearing up. "Lynn you are the shit G. real talk. I appreciate this chance but I gotta decline. I just found out I'm pregnant!"

"Congrats!" Everyone yelled. "I also got accepted into dental school, so I just want to quit the game and do right yall. Lynn please don't be mad."

I sat quietly and let her finish her speech. It was definitely a shock that she was pregnant because no one us were seeing anyone seriously.

"Nikki, that's the plan. To do right. I would never be mad at you for choosing you're unborn over us. I'm so proud of you and I hope all of us take a page out of your book and continue our higher education one day.

You know I'm throwing that baby shower right!" I threw in there so she would believe I really was genuinely happy for her.

"I'm the God mother right bitch?" Tru asked. Nikki rolled her eyes and said "Of course!"

"Lynn don't try to outdo us and bring all those damn totes to the baby shower either."

"Bitch stay going to people's shit with totes full of clothes, pampers, shoes and shit."

"What the fuck they even need the baby shower for, if she going to buy everything!!" they all cracked up laughing at Lynn's expense.

And that's how Christmas night ended. Full of laughs and memories. No one knew that it would be their last time celebrating this holiday together under one roof.

Chapter 26

Boom Boom Boom! "Open up, it's the FBI!" After hearing the front door flying off the hinges, my eyes popped open and at that moment I was glad I fell asleep in my clothes from the day before.

Before I could put on my shoes the door was kicked off the hinges and before I could blink my face was hitting the floor and my arms were put roughly behind my back!

My house was swarming with federal agents and hell of police. Scared wasn't the word!

To Be Continued

Team Concrete: The Players

CHAPTER 1.

Lynn

It seems like as the days go by things get worse and worse. All the phone calls I'm getting now are of the girls saying there cards aren't working. I'm replacing more stuff than money I'm making, and to make it even worse peoples gift cards are turning off before they make it to the store.

Viv

"Sister Sister where are you where are you?" I yelled into the phone once Lynn picked up.

"I'm on the north side, what's wrong? Why do you sound like that?" She quizzed me.

Out of breath I spoke "I had to jump out of my window. The police were at my door. I don't know what's going on I'm scared! Come get me!!" I banged on my friend's apartment in the building next to mine.

"Oh my god! What? You jumped out of the window from your second floor apartment?"

"Yes yes I had to," I said breathing hard and my knee is killing me. I'm hiding in someone else's apartment please hurry and call me back," and she hung up.

Lynn

"Tru what the fuck is going on? I just got a call from Viv and she had to jump out her window?" I asked Tru, silently praying they were playing a cruel joke on me.

"I know I know. Hell I'm the one who answered the door. I thought it was her worker coming by. She..."

"Wait hold up! Back up, her worker? When? Where? How? I'm so lost and I'm getting mad Tru!" I said as calm as I could without getting to heated at Tru.
She listens to me but won't hesitate to snap the hell back.

"Remember ol girl who grew up with us next door on Cottage Grove? Me and her were always together."

"Yeah a little bit," I responded trying to jog my memory.

"What she got to do with anything?" I asked.

"Well she came back around and started working for Viv. She called to say she was on her way, so when somebody knocked at the door I thought it

130

was her and went to open the door. Well I'm glad I said who is it and they responded Will County Detectives looking for Vivian Donaldson." Tru said out of breath.

O no I thought, but I didn't express it to Tru. I didn't need them worried too soon. 1st that damn dream three weeks ago about the feds busting in my crib and now this shit. Was it the sign I ignored. Fuck!!

"Wait a minute, so what do you think? You think she's been set up or some shit? That's her worker? When did she get some workers? What the fuck is going on? What's ol girl name Tru?

"Courtney."